Sturdy, tireless Rod Damon gives his all to prevent a band of beautiful hippies from turning the government onto an all-time high—on LSD.

From the tips of their sandled feet to the tops of their lovely acid-heads, these chicks are in a white heat of rebellion. And Rod Damon is the only man with enough cool to quench their fiery demands.

Set against New York's psychedelic East Village scene, A HARD ACT TO FOLLOW is a racy romp through the beds of the kookiest enemy agents ever to drop out of The Great Society!

Published By
WARNER PAPERBACK LIBRARY

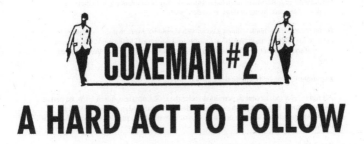

COXEMAN #2

A HARD ACT TO FOLLOW

AN ADULT NOVEL BY BY TROY CONWAY

POPULAR LIBRARY

Copyright © 1968 by Hachette Book Group USA

Popular Library
Hachette Book Group USA
237 Park Avenue
New York, NY 10017

Popular Library is an imprint of Grand Central Publishing. The Popular Library name and logo is a trademark of Hachette Book Group USA, Inc. The Coxeman name and logo is a trademark of Hachette Book Group USA, Inc.

Visit our Web site at www.HachetteBookGroupUSA.com

First Printing: January 1968

Cover photograph by Cosimo

Printed in the United States of America

Conway, Troy
Hard Act to Follow, A / Troy Conway
(Coxeman, #2)

ISBN 0-446-54311-X / 978-0-446-54311-8

CHAPTER 1

Her name was Lola, and her game was love.

She was, in other words, a hippie—a member of the vast underground army of bearded guys and long-haired dolls who burst on the American scene in the last few years and waged war on The Establishment using the one weapon that no one ever has been able to defend himself against: love.

She was a hippie and she wanted love.

And I wasn't about to challenge her, especially since the present object of her affections happened to be me.

My name's Damon, Rod Damon. Or, more precisely, *Dr*. Rod Damon.

I hold a Ph.D. in sociology and I'm an associate professor at a major university in the northeastern United States.

Also, I'm founder, director and chief researcher for the League for Sexual Dynamics.

The League is more of a pleasure than a business. It's something I conceived during my pre-doctoral days when I was trying to figure out a way to have my sociological cake and eat it too.

I applied for grants from knowledge-hungry foundations and used the money to research the sexual mores of various segments of contemporary society. My findings have been published in all the major journals, earning me a reputation as one of the country's most distinguished behavioral scientists.

5

And my field studies have brought me into contact with some of the grooviest chicks ever hatched. As Benny Goodman might have put it, nice work if you can get it.

My first project was a study of the sexual behavior of American coeds.

My next was a study of parallels between sexual behavior of American coeds and contemporary non-college females.

Subsequently I studied the sexual behavior of female graduate students, of female Ph.D.'s, of female college dropouts, of suburban housewives, of urban housewives, of rural housewives, of New York career girls, of Los Angeles career girls, of Washington (D.C.) career girls, of London career girls, of Paris career girls, of Rome career girls and of prostitutes in West German brothels.

Then I began studying the sexual behavior of female hippies.

As I described the project on the application to the foundation which financed it, I intended to investigate: "(a) motivational factors operative among females of the so-called 'hippie' community in the selection of males to whom they relate sexually; (b) characteristics of the males so selected; and (c) the nature and extent of sexual practices which transpire once selection has been made."

Translating the jargonese into English, I wanted to know who the hippie chicks swung with, why they swung with them, and how they swung—especially how.

To find out, I went to New York's East Village, rented a coldwater flat, stopped shaving, let my hair grow and bought a closetful of second hand clothes. In short, I made every effort to become assimilated into bearded, hippie society. That's how I met Lola.

It happened in a bar on St. Mark's Place—a crazy psychedelicatessen where strobe lights play hell with your vision, twanging guitars play hell with your hearing, and pushy bartenders play hell with your bankroll.

6

I'd been researching the joint without a bite for more than three ear-shattering hours when she sauntered in, looked around and made a beeline to where I was sitting.

"Want to make it?" she asked.

"Huh?" I replied, caught off guard by her approach.

"DO YOU WANT TO MAKE IT?" she repeated, this time loud enough for the entire bar to hear. And just in case there was some doubt in my mind as to what she was talking about, she ran her tongue around her full, red lips like a scene out of the Tom Jones movie.

Her bluntness should not have caught me off guard. I'd been in the East Village for nearly three weeks, and I knew that hippies like to get to the point without any preliminaries.

But Lola was no run-of-the-mill, flat-on-top, flabby-on-bottom, frayed-at-the-edges, down-at-the-heels hippie.

She was an eye-popping, mind-blowing, passion-provoking picture of pulchritude—an exciting super-chick with a face like a Botticelli madonna and a body that made it hard for a guy to think about her as just a simple flower child.

Her eyes were ice-blue and her hair was moonlight-gold. Her moist, pink lips sheathed a set of pearl-white teeth that was a promise of things to come. Beneath her baggy shirt was a full bosom and the skin-tight, cut-off blue jeans that hugged her hips and thighs left nothing to the imagination.

"Your pad or mine?" I asked.

She wrinkled her nose, and the corners of her mouth darted downward in a saucy little pout. She groaned. "If we've got to have a big debate about it, forget it."

"My pad," I said, polishing off the remains of a Scotch and soda. "It's right around the corner."

A few minutes later we were in the fourth-floor walk-up penthouse of the tumbled-down tenement I called home, and a few minutes later we were in bed.

Undressed, Lola looked even better than she had with

7

her clothes on. Her milk-white breasts were impressively large, admirably high and as firm as a pair of sun-ripened melons. In the center of each was a pink rosette and a distended nipple. Beneath, her waist tapered gently into what had to be the most curvaceous hips in creativity, and her long golden legs were a sweet promise.

But she didn't give me much time to admire the view. No sooner had I shucked the last of my duds than her hands were on me—probing, pulling, tugging, squeezing. Her kiss was a cushion of velvet and her love play became a crescendo of passion. Her tongue, a tip of fire, flickered at my navel, my chest, my thighs and the tip of my passion. Then she moved on top of me. Her womanhood contacted me like a thousand hungry tongues. Her legs shot forward in a trembling letter-V, then closed around my head, clutching me to her. She writhed frantically like a jockey. Then our bodies fell into a passionate rhythm of the act.

Her eyes were shut, and her face was screwed up in an expression of exquisite pain-pleasure. She moaned and mumbled.

I frankly wondered just what the hell she was talking about, but I didn't give it very much thought. The sensations she was stirring inside me were far more interesting.

Her body quivered with excitement and her fingernails dug feverishly into the muscles of my shoulders.

"Love me!" she gasped, "Love me!" Then, digging her knees into the mattress, she pressed her advantage. The force of the attack made me tremble and twitch. She leaned over and dug her teeth into my neck, and my back arched high into the air. I grabbed her by the hair, jerked her head back and violently kissed her mouth. Then my fingers found their way along her sides until they had a tight grip on her writhing, squirming buttocks. I pushed against her with all the strength I could muster.

"Love me!" she cried.

8

With studied casualness, I slowed the tempo to a lazy largo. Taking her legs in my arms, I lifted them high above her body, almost bending her in two. Then I teased her as I came to a halt. She opened her eyes. Then I was off again up to the hilt. At the same time, my mouth found her left breast and I bit hard into it.

"Oooooohhhhh, baby! You're killing me! I can't stand it!"

Each piston stroke sent new ripples of excitement through her luscious, trembling body. Each ripple produced another desperate groan.

Finally she could take it no longer. Hooking her calves around my buttocks she squeezed me against her and we rolled over. Her mouth found mine. She thrust once, twice, a third time. Then, with loud gasps and together, we abandoned ourselves to the sweet, shattering spasms of climax.

When it was over, she lay limply beneath me. "Like, wow," she said wearily. "And I thought you were a square."

I let the compliment go unacknowledged. It wasn't that I was unappreciative. It was that I'd learned in my travels around the East Village that hippies place a premium on playing it cool. "Why this free sex?" I asked, casually changing the subject. "Like, since when is sex a charity affair?"

She buried her face against my neck, and her fingers toyed playfully with my hair. "Well, you know," she murmured affectionately. "I mean, it's all part of the movement and everything. I mean, it's the thing to do."

My furrowed brow told her that I didn't have the vaguest idea of what she was talking about.

"I mean," she went on, "you're not from around here, are you? I mean, you're a tourist."

"In a manner of speaking," I conceded, failing to see the connection.

"I knew that you were a tourist as soon as I saw you. I

9

mean, when I came into the bar and saw you sitting there with your drink, I just knew you couldn't be one of us. You looked okay and you were dressed okay, but I could tell you really weren't part of the scene."

"Then why'd you come over to me?"

"That's the whole point. I wanted to turn you on, you know?"

"No, I don't know. Like you said, I'm a tourist."

She slithered over to the side of the bed and tugged a pack of Kents from the pocket of her jeans, which were heaped on top of her shirt and sandals on the floor. "Well," she explained, "the key to the whole hippie movement is love. I mean, that's what's wrong with the world. There isn't enough love in it. People get all hung up on materialism, and they forget the basics. You know?"

"An interesting analysis," I admitted.

"Well, it isn't original. I got it from The Big Head, and he got it from philosophers of ages past."

"The Big Head. Who's he?"

"Who's *he*? Just the high priest of the Church of the Sacred Acid, that's all. You mean you never heard of him?"

"Now that you mention it, the man sounds familiar."

"Pretty soon there won't be a person alive who doesn't know who he is. He's going to be one of the foremost leaders of all time."

"I'll take your word for it, but I still don't see what this has to do with me."

"Well, not long ago I was a self-centered, spoiled little brat. I mean, my parents had bread and I got everything I wanted. I had my own car and all kinds of clothes and even my own private telephone, and I lived in a decadent, materialistic suburb on the North Shore. Get the picture?"

"So far, yeah."

"Anyway, I started running with the Village crowd. That's when I discovered grass and acid and everything.

10

Then I heard one of The Big Head's sermons. That's when I found out where things were really at."

"Stop the train. I know that grass is marijuana and acid is LSD, but how could sermons teach you where things are at?"

"*You* know. I mean, it's *love* and everything. The Big Head showed me that my car and my clothes and my private telephone were all part of the materialistic rat race. Like, they're not important. All that's important is love."

"And that's why you went to bed with me?"

"Exactly! I mean, now that The Big Head showed me where it's at, all I think about is love. Whenever I meet a lonely somebody, I try to give him all the love I have. When I saw you in the bar, sitting there looking deprived and everything, I knew you needed love. So I went up to you and told you you could have me. I mean, that's the way the whole world should be. If it was, there wouldn't be any wars or poverty or anything, would there?"

"Perhaps not," I granted. "Anyway, thanks. And I'm glad you enjoyed it as much as I did."

"Oh, I did! It was beautiful! You really have a lot of love in you. You ought to stop by the Church sometime. The Big Head would really dig meeting you. You'd be such an asset to the movement."

"I'll make it a point to look him up tomorrow. Meanwhile, speaking of love . . . ," I started saying, then rubbed her belly, obviously at the ready.

"You do have a lot of love in you. I never met anyone with so much love to give away."

Actually I hadn't pooped out because I'm afflicted with a bizarre variety of the physiological disorder known as priapism. In other words, I practically have a perpetual erection.

Most priapists suffer a fate worse than death. While they're constantly rarin'-to-go, they can't do anything once they get there. That is, they don't experience orgasm. It's

11

sort of like owning a sleek new automobile that can't be taken out of the garage.

I'm different. Thanks to Fate, biology or what-have-you, I'm not only ready to go, I'm fully capable of enjoying the trip. Medical science calls the situation unique. I call it groovy.

Of course, I didn't bother explaining all this to Lola. If she wanted to attribute my stamina to an abundance of love, I wasn't going to try to change her mind. I began kissing her lightly on the lips, neck, bosom, and other interesting places. She began to kiss me all over, discovering new erogenous zones. Then I proceeded to take up where we had left off a few minutes before.

But this time things didn't go quite so smoothly.

No sooner had we started moving than she stopped cold. Her eyes went glassy, and her face went pale. Her body stiffened.

"What's wrong?" I asked.

"Unnhhh," she replied, her voice filled with fright.

"Huh?"

"*Unnnnhhhhhh!!!*"

I touched her face. It was rigid.

Finally I slapped her lightly across the cheek. She found her voice. "Behind you!" she whispered urgently. "Look what's behind you!"

CHAPTER 2

I looked.

Then I looked again.

No wonder she had said "what" and not "who."

Fortunately I hadn't taken any mind-expanding drugs or I might've thought I was flipping out. Even without drugs I found it hard to believe I hadn't popped my cork.

The guy was tall, gaunt and lean as a swizzle stick. Judging from the wrinkles in his weather-beaten face, his age was sixty-plus. Judging from the bags under his eyes, he hadn't slept for months.

He wore an orange leather shirt, madras bermuda shorts and calf-high black riding boots. Hanging from his neck was a heavy silver Iron Cross. Rounding out the ensemble was a pair of blue-tinted, steel-rimmed glasses—the kind Benjamin Franklin used to favor. And, as if this get-up weren't weird enough, he also was wearing what had to be the most obvious hairpiece ever assembled.

A very familiar smile peeked out from under his walrus-like mustache. "Good evening, Damon," he said amiably. "I hope I'm not interrupting."

It's a good thing blood doesn't really boil, or mine would have. "Interrupting!" I thundered. "What could possibly make you think you're interrupting?"

His smile broadened and the ends of his walrus-moustache danced playfully in front of his yellow, horse-like teeth. "Well, in my line of work, one often gets the

13

feeling that people aren't happy to see one. I suppose one becomes slightly paranoid after a time."

"Also slightly rude." I nodded toward Lola, who was still lying stiff as a corpse beneath me. "You frightened the poor girl out of her wits. Couldn't you have waited until we were finished?"

"Knowing you, that might not have been for days. In my line of work, every minute counts. Besides, you left your door unlocked In my line of work——"

"Yeah, I know. In your line of work, an unlocked door is an engraved invitation."

His line of work, as I had discovered some time before, was espionage He was a high-ranking representative of an all-powerful, top-secret and, so far as I could discern, nameless U.S government agency which specialized in saving the world from the forces of tyranny.

One night, a pair of goons on the agency payroll had busted into my apartment, pulled me out of the arms of a pretty girl, and spirited me off to a tractor-trailer which served as his mobile field office.

He then asked me to infiltrate a brothel at Hamburg, Germany, under the pretext of conducting a sexual study for the Thaddeus X. Coxe foundation. If I said no, I might have been prosecuted for statutory rape, fornication, adultery, Mann Act violations and sundry other sex crimes connected with my research projects. Also income tax evasion, stemming from certain discrepancies in the bookkeeping system of the League for Sexual Dynamics.

So, reluctantly, I became a Thaddeus X. Coxe-man— and an American agent. My mission was to get information on a quartet of neo-Nazi nuts who were plotting to lure the United States into nuclear war with Russia and China.

I wasn't too happy about the job, but I did it—and if I must say so myself, I did it pretty well. Several months and several thousand bullets after I had come on the scene, the plot had been foiled and the plotters were all dead or

14

behind bars. That, I had assumed, was the last I would see of Walrus-moustache.

But there he was again.

"Well," I sighed wearily, "what is it this time? More nasty Nazis threatening the world?"

"Not quite. But something equally sinister." He fished a tiny pillcase out of his shirt pocket and handed me a bullet-shaped blue capsule. "Here," he said. "Give this to your girlfriend. It'll send her on a trip she'll really enjoy. By the time she comes back, you and I will have discussed all our business and I'll be on my way back to Washington."

I examined the capsule. "What is it? LSD?"

"Something similar. It's called LSP—'P' as in 'Pronto!' It works faster than LSD, and its effects are shorter-lived but far more intense." He gestured impatiently. "Now hurry up and give it to her. There's no time to waste."

I didn't argue. It would have been futile. What do you say to a guy who has enough on you to put you behind bars for the rest of your life? You say "yes," that's what you say. Walrus-moustache and I both knew it.

Beneath me, Lola was stirring slightly. I put the capsule between my lips, then kissed her open mouth. "Turn-on time, honey," I said. Obediently she took the capsule and swallowed it.

"Now watch," Walrus-moustache told me. "In seconds your shock-stricken princess is going to become one of the most sexually aroused girls you've ever seen."

As if on cue, Lola sprung vigorously into action. Her arms clasped my back, and her calves locked around the underside of my knees. Her hips darted back and forth like a pair of well-oiled pistons.

"Oh, wow!" she moaned. "Wow, wow, wow, wow, wow!!!"

Then it was over. Panting like a dog on a hot summer day, she lay limply beneath me. I felt like I had just run the three-minute mile.

15

"Well, so much for that," Walrus-moustache observed nonchalantly. He sat on the edge of the bed. "Now to get down to business."

"Is she asleep?"

"Not exactly, but she's so wrapped up in her thoughts that she won't pay the slightest attention to what we're saying. In fact, when she comes down off her trip, she won't even remember I was here. All she'll know is that she just made love like she's never made love before."

"She knew that the first time I made love to her."

"Well, now she'll know it even better. You may have a hard time getting rid of her. She'll probably chase you all over the Village hoping for another date."

"That LSP must be quite a pill."

"It is. Like they say, groovier living through chemistry." He permitted himself a small smile. "But," he added quickly, "I didn't come here to help in your conquests. We've got work to do. Mix me a drink. It's been a long night, and I need one."

Frankly, I needed one too. Slipping on a bathrobe, I made my way to the kitchen and poured two Scotches—his on the rocks, mine with soda. "Okay," I said, "what're we up to this time?"

He stared pensively at his glass. His jaw tightened, and beneath his ludicrous toupee I could see lines of worry etched across his forehead. "Damon," he replied softly after a moment, "we're in trouble. Our beloved country—your country and mine—is presently facing one of the gravest crises in its two-hundred-year history. Unless we act quickly, and wisely, we may lose the cherished freedoms we have come to regard as our natural birthright."

I chuckled in spite of myself. The sight of a sixty-year-old man dressed like a hippie and mouthing patriotic speeches was more than I could take with a straight face. "You sound like a re-run of one of those World War II movies starring John Wayne," I told him.

16

His frown made it clear that he didn't appreciate my sense of humor. "Don't underestimate the seriousness of the situation," he said somberly. "If we can't get to the bottom of this thing soon, the entire Free World may fall into the hands of the enemy."

"Which enemy? Russia? Red China? North Vietnam? Or do we have one I haven't heard of yet?"

"We don't know. We suspect Red China, but we aren't sure. In fact, we aren't sure of anything—except the way they plan to take over our government."

"And how might that be?"

He lowered his voice to a near-whisper. "A coup, Damon. Can you believe that? A coup?"

"A *coup d'etat?* A forceful military seizure?"

"Precisely."

"By the Red Chinese?"

"By the hippies—with Red Chinese backing."

I stared at him incredulously. "You've got to be kidding."

"I wish I were."

"But how could they pull it off? The United States isn't a little banana republic with four or five men at the seat of power. We've got fifty autonomous states and the biggest federal bureaucracy in the history of the world. Lately our lawfully elected representatives have had trouble keeping things under control. How could a band of insurgents— hippies, at that—hope to manage it?"

"Maybe they couldn't. But in a way, they'll succeed even if they fail. Does that sound confusing?"

"Very."

"Then perhaps I should start at the beginning."

"By all means do."

He took a long swallow of Scotch and drummed idly on the glass with his fingertips. "Some months ago, we began receiving reports from one of our agents in Hong Kong that the Red Chinese were planning to infiltrate the hippie

17

movement. We were told that Mao's intelligence people had placed unlimited funds at the disposal of the would-be infiltrators and that Operation Hippie had been given priority over all other espionage projects. No one seemed to know why the hippies suddenly had become so interesting to the Chinese. But our agent swore that the sources of information were unimpeachable. So we followed up on the lead. We had several of our best people mingle in with the hippies and find out everything they could."

"What did they find out?"

"Not much. So far as we could discern, the affairs of the hippies were moving along quite normally. There were pot parties, LSD trips, antiwar demonstrations and free-love communes—in short, everything The Establishment frowns on. But nothing in the least bit suggestive of a Chinese infiltration. Finally we pulled our people off the job."

"Then all hell broke loose."

"How did you know?"

"That's the way it always happens in spy movies."

"Ah, yes. Art invariably mimics reality. Anyway, about a week after our people left the scene, a young man sought treatment at a San Francisco public health clinic while suffering the ill effects of a bad LSD trip. Under the care of a physician from the Department of Health, Education and Welfare, whose report found its way to our files, the fellow spoke of a plot called 'The Big Freak-Out.' According to him, a group of hippies was conspiring to take over the United States by polluting the water supply of Washington, D.C., with a heavy concentration of LSD. Presumably the conspirators believed that the entire city—including the President, the Congress and the Cabinet—would go off on a twenty-four-hour acid trip. Then while everyone was freaked-out the coup would take place. One of the hippies would declare himself President, others would take over the Cabinet positions and still others

18

would occupy the lower rungs on the administrative ladder. In short, the entire executive branch of government would be under the control of the conspirators."

"Incredible!"

"We thought so too. In fact, we had all but dismissed the whole thing as a wild acid-head's dream. Then, a few days later, another bad-trip hippie sought treatment at a clinic in New York. He told substantially the same story. A few days after that, a third hippie described the very same plot at a clinic in Chicago. Three bad-trip hippies in three different cities, all telling the same tale. Rather disconcerting, don't you think?"

"Maybe the whole thing was a hoax, like that banana business. Remember, the hippies had the whole country convinced that banana peels were hallucinogenic before the F.D.A. exploded the myth."

"Possible, but unlikely. First of all, the three hippies were in the advanced stages of a drug-induced psychosis. To have told a calculated lie while in that condition would have been next to impossible. Secondly, the F.B.I. has all but ruled out collusion. Our people ordered a full-scale investigation and there wasn't a shred of evidence that any of the three hippies knew either of the other two. Third, and most significant, all three are now dead. The San Francisco fellow was killed in San Francisco, the New York fellow in New York and the Chicago fellow in St. Louis—all within a few days of each other. In every case, death was the result of garroting—or more precisely, strangulation with a strand of piano wire. Incidentally, garroting is one of the favorite murder methods of Red Chinese agents."

"But if the three hippies didn't know each other, how could they have been working together? And if they weren't working together, why were they killed?"

"Elementary, my dear Damon. All three could have been underlings in the conspiracy, none known to the other

19

two, yet all known to parties higher up in the hierarchy. Recent developments argue very strongly in favor of that possibility."

"What recent developments?"

"Since the third fellow was killed, there have been four other piano wire strangulations that we know about—two in New York, one in San Francisco and one in Miami. All took place in the same week. The victims in each case were hippies, and three of the four had visited public health clinics for treatment of a bad trip shortly before their deaths."

"Did they say anything about The Big Freak-Out?"

"No. But, don't you see, they *could* have. It all fits into place."

"I don't follow you."

"Well, let's presume for a moment that there *is* a plot to overthrow the government—a vast and insidious conspiracy involving a sizable number of hippies in half a dozen different cities. Suddenly one of the hippies takes a bad trip and seeks treatment at a public health clinic. No one knows what he said while he was there. But everyone knows what he *could* have said. So the higher-ups decide that he can't be trusted in the future, because he obviously can't hold his acid. They kill him. Then another hippie takes a bad trip and visits a clinic, and he's killed too. Then a third, then a fourth, and so on. By this time, word has spread that it's very dangerous for a conspirator to visit a public health clinic. So the visits stop, and so do the killings. It all adds up, doesn't it?"

"Yes, assuming there actually is a plot. I'm not convinced that there is."

"Then consider the alternatives. Suppose there isn't a plot. That leaves us with the question of how three bad-trip hippies could have told the same story at three public health clinics in three different cities—three hippies who didn't know each other and who were too far flipped-out to

20

tell a calculated lie. Coincidence? Unlikely. A hoax? We've already ruled that out. What other possibilities are there?"

"I can't think of any," I admitted.

"Next, there's the question of why these three hippies, and the four who didn't talk, were all killed—and all with the same style murder weapon. Coincidence? Impossible."

"Maybe it was the Mafia. They've been trafficking in LSD lately. Suppose the seven murdered guys had bought their acid from Mafia sources and were killed so they couldn't identify their suppliers?"

"Conceivable, but unlikely. For one thing, the Mafia doesn't go in for garroting. For another, if they rubbed out every guy they supplied who had a bad trip and visited a public health clinic, they'd have to kill a lot more than just seven men." He shook his head sadly. "No, Damon, it isn't the Mafia. And since it obviously isn't coincidence, the possibilities are narrowed down to one: a Chinese-sponsored Big Freak-Out."

"You argue a good case," I granted. "Still, I'm skeptical. First of all, I can't see how Chinamen could infiltrate a Caucasian group without giving themselves away. The racial differences are pretty obvious, aren't they? Secondly, I don't like this business about the garrote. If the Chinese Reds actually are behind a plot to overthrow our government, they'll want to keep their participation as secret as possible. So why kill seven men with a murder weapon that focuses suspicion directly on them?"

He smiled faintly. "Both objections are valid, Damon. In fact, I've pondered them myself long before our meeting tonight. As to the first, we can only assume that the Chinese are using Caucasian operatives—perhaps Americans who are taking orders from a Chinese source, or maybe Europeans or Latins who're working in the same manner. As to the second, your guess is as good as mine. Maybe the Chinaman in charge of the operation is too stupid to realize that we'd associate garroting with the

21

Chinese. Or maybe he's playing a game of counterpsychology—using a weapon which is obviously Chinese so we'll assume that the plotters actually represent another nation which wants to cast suspicion on the Chinese. Whatever the case, the evidence now at hand points very definitely toward Chinese involvement."

"By 'evidence' I take it you mean that report from your agent in Hong Kong."

"That's part of it, but there's more. For example, during recent months there's been a slackening off of Chinese spy activity all over the globe. That could mean that Mao's espionage people have suddenly been put on an austerity program, or it could mean that China's previous expansionist policies are being revised. But it could also mean that funds and personnel are being diverted from conventional spy areas to unconventional spy areas—like The Big Freak-Out. Also, the American underground newspapers —those kooky weeklies and bi-weeklies that circulate among hippies in most of the big cities—have been running a lot of articles lately which are highly sympathetic to Mao, to other Chinese leaders, and to the Chinese way of life in general. This could be just an extension of the leftist and pro-mystic line these papers have always followed. Or it could mean that Mao's public relations people are paving the way for a more overt hippie-commie alliance. Over the past few months we've had nearly a dozen similar indications that the Chinese and the hippies are walking hand in hand. No one indication is a conclusive link, but put them all together and they're pretty persuasive."

He drained his drink and handed me the glass for a refill. I poured us each a stiff one.

"All right," I said once we were re-situated, "let's say the Chinese *are* behind the plot. Didn't you agree earlier that the chances of a successful coup are next to nil?"

"No. I agreed that the hippies might not be able to run

the country once they seized power. I never said they wouldn't be able to seize it."

"But how? We've got a Secret Service and an enormous standing army. Then there's the FBI, the Washington police force, the National Guard, the Army Reserve and——"

"And every last man-jack of them drinks water."

"Oh, yeah," I remembered. "That's where the LSD comes in."

"Exactly." He took a healthy slug of Scotch, then toyed with the ice cubes in his glass. "LSD is one of the most perfect chemical compounds ever synthesized. It's colorless, odorless and tasteless. When dissolved in water or some other liquid, it can't be detected except by laboratory analysis involving the most sophisticated equipment. Two hundred and fifty micrograms are enough to make a person hallucinate. One milligram can send the most jaded acid-head on a trip to end all trips. And one kilogram could turn on the whole city of Washington, D.C., and all its suburbs."

I whistled under my breath.

"Of course," he added quickly, "the plan isn't without certain bugs. For one thing, the hippies will have to put enough LSD into the Potomac River to insure that everyone in Washington consumes at least a threshold dose. That means computing the total amount of water which flows in one day and the total amount actually consumed by the people, either through drinking or absorption into cooked foods. Also they'll have to come up with some sort of additive to insure that the LSD won't be vitiated between the time it's put into the river and the time the water reaches the people's homes. But the first problem can be solved by simple mathematics and the second by chemistry. Our laboratory people have solved them both, and since the hippies had a head start on us, it's safe to assume that they've solved them too—or soon will."

23

"Is it also safe to assume that once the LSD has been put into the Potomac there's no way to foil the plot?"

"There's no way. Our people presently are trying to develop an antidote which would render the drug impotent, but so far they haven't come up with anything. Moreover, even if we had an antidote, it would be useless unless we knew precisely *when* the river would be polluted." The furrows in his brow deepened. "So, as things now stand, we're pretty much at the mercy of the hippies. Somewhere between twenty-four and forty-eight hours after they pollute the Potomac, the entire city will be freaked out. And when that happens—well, I shudder to think of the consequences."

I shuddered with him.

"Imagine it, Damon," he went on, his eyes bulging as if the foreseen spectacle had suddenly begun to unfold in front of him. "It's seven a.m. and the nation's capital is beginning another routine day. People sit down at the breakfast table and drink concentrated orange juice—made with water. They eat eggs—poached in water. They drink coffee—boiled with water. Then they go off to work and the hallucinations begin. Motorists drive off the expressways. Pedestrians throw fits in the middle of the streets. At the White House the President is meeting with the Secretary of State. Suddenly one of them imagines that he can fly and dives through a plate glass window. The other sits back and digs the sound of the breaking glass. On Capitol Hill, the Senate is in session. Suddenly the majority leader becomes infatuated with the frescos on the chamber ceiling and the minority whip begins turning cartwheels up and down the aisles. In the House and at the Pentagon, the story is more or less the same. Legislators forget their legislation and listen to the beautiful music being played inside their heads. Generals make paper airplanes or pelt each other with spitballs. By noon every man, woman and child in the greater Washington area is high as the

24

proverbial kite. They eat more and they drink more, and they get higher still. Meanwhile, somewhere on the outskirts of the city, perhaps in Arlington or Bethesda or Chevy Chase, the Red Chinese-controlled hippies have a small army—an inexpensive army—waiting to make a big move. At dusk they go into action. One platoon advances on the White House. The leader declares himself President, an underling declares himself Vice-President and another underling declares himself Chief of the Secret Service. No one offers any opposition, because everyone is too flipped out to really care. At the Pentagon, another platoon makes its move. The leader declares himself Secretary of Defense, an underling declares himself Chairman of the Joint Chiefs of Staff, four others take command of the Army, Navy, Air Force and Marines. Orders are dispatched to all military commands to cease all activity until further notice. Again there is no opposition; the Pentagon staff is freaked out, and the commanders in the field have no choice but to follow orders. In Foggy Bottom, another platoon takes over the State Department. On Constitution Avenue, still another takes over the Treasury. The radio and TV people know what's happening, but their reports to the outside world are totally incomprehensible. Ditto the newspaper people and their reports—if anybody reports anything at all. In short, the capital has been cut off from the rest of the country, and chaos reigns supreme."

I forced a smile. "Well, sophisticates have always complained that Washington was a dead town. I guess they'll have to revise their opinion."

He stared into space as if he hadn't heard me. "Soon," he continued, "newsmen in other cities will realize that something has happened. They'll investigate. But the investigators will suffer the same fate as the Washington residents. The effects of the LSD will linger for days. Chickens who have drunk the polluted water will lay polluted eggs. Bottling plants will dispense cases of polluted

25

soft drinks. Cows will give polluted milk—all this presupposing that there's some egg-laying, soft drink-dispensing and milk-giving to begin with. Meanwhile, there'll be nothing to prevent the Chinese from dropping a few bombs on us, or on anyone else we're presently protecting. With our military operations at a standstill and our seat of government wholly immobilized, who's to stop her? And Russia can get into the act too. She's been pretty friendly lately, but I for one suspect strongly that her friendliness is the result of fear. With our military capabilities reduced to nothing, she'd have no reason to be afraid anymore. Nor would anyone else. Even Albania could take a shot at us. Or Castro. We'd be sitting ducks for everyone who hates us. And as you know, their number is legion."

"You turn a nice cliché," I put in.

He continued to stare into space, oblivious of my presence. "Eventually, of course, the effects of the drug would wear off, and order would be restored. The insurrectionist hippies would be put behind bars, and our lawful leaders would resume command. But by this time the damage would have been done. Our cities—those of them that hadn't been bombed out of existence—would be veritable seas of confusion. The stock market would have crashed. The armed forces would have become completely neutralized. Industrial progress would have ground to a halt. On the international scene, all but the staunchest of our allies—namely South Korea, Australia and New Zealand—would have deserted us. The neutralist nations would regard us with contempt, the communist bloc with scorn. Kosygin would herald the fall of capitalism which Marx and Lenin so long ago predicted. De Gaulle would tell us that he had told us so. America would have lost, perhaps for all time, her position as leader of the Free World." He polished off his drink in one quick swallow. "Indeed, there might not be a Free World anymore."

26

I took his empty glass and poured refills for both of us. When I returned, the faraway look had left his eyes. He took the fresh drink, sipped it and looked up at me, as if waiting for a barrage of questions.

I didn't have any questions, but I did have a few objections. "From where I sit," I told him, "it looks like the success of the plot hinges on its remaining secret. Now that you know, what's to stop you from alerting everyone concerned not to drink the water."

He chuckled. "Easily said, Damon, but not so easily done. Actually, we've set up a program that would keep the President, the Vice President, the Joint Chiefs of Staff and other key figures from drinking polluted water. The way it would work, everyone on our list would only drink water and eat foods prepared with water which has been analyzed for chemical content. But obviously there's a limit to the number of people we can put on the list. And even if everyone on the list obeyed our instructions, the pollution maneuver still would have devastating effects. The hippies might not seize the White House, the Pentagon, the State Department and the Treasury. But they'd wreak havoc on the rest of the government."

"Still, the plot would be foiled."

"Maybe. Unfortunately, though, the powers that be aren't very interested in our program."

"What do you mean?"

"Well, I hadn't intended to involve you in inter-agency politics, but the fact is that our people haven't enjoyed the President's good graces lately. To put it mildly, we're in the White House doghouse. I won't go into details, but suffice it to say that we've suffered a few defeats in other operations we've conducted recently, and now we're on The Man's S-list."

"I get the point."

"Anyway, the White House isn't very interested in what we have to say anymore. In fact, there's even been some

27

talk of disbanding our agency."

"Then the President doesn't believe that this plot is underway, and he refuses to take precautions of any sort. Is that what you're telling me?"

"He not only doesn't believe it, he doesn't even know about it. The Cabinet officer to whom the head of our agency is responsible refuses to tell him unless we can provide convincing proof that we're not just letting our imaginations run away with us."

"What kind of proof does he want?"

"That remains to be seen. All we know is that nothing we've told him so far—including everything I told you, and then some—has had any effect. Meanwhile, official Washington goes its usual way, totally unaware of the dangers which lurk right around the proverbial corner."

I swallowed hard. "In other words, the hippies—or whoever is behind them—are getting ready to make their move. When they make it, it'll be the end of the Free World. And our side can't even take precautions to minimize the effects of the plot because one pigheaded Cabinet officer distrusts your agency."

"Precisely."

"So what's the next move?"

He smiled conspiratorially. "The agency does the same thing it did when it had problems with the neo-Nazis in Hamburg, Damon. It calls on you to pull its chestnuts out of the fire."

"But what can I do?"

"Well, for openers, you can infiltrate the hippies. Mix in with them, talk to them, share their ideas. That shouldn't be too much of a problem, because you're already living among them. Thanks to your credentials as a sex researcher, they'll accept you, and they'll speak freely to you— or at least they'll speak more freely than they would to a conventional espionage type."

28

"So far, so good. But what do I do once they accept me."

"You find out anything and everything you can about The Big Freak-Out. That won't be easy, but it shouldn't be impossible either. If they plan the sort of militarist caper which we project, there'll have to be at least three or four hundred of them involved. Since hippies aren't by nature a conspiratorial lot, a few of the three or four hundred should be rather loose-mouthed. Your job is to connect with them, pry what information you can from them and report everything to me."

"And that's all there is to it?"

"Not quite. You see, if you can supply me with enough evidence to persuade the Cabinet officer to whom our agency is responsible that the plot is actually in the works, we'll be able to sell the President on our program to minimize the effects of the pollution maneuver. But the maneuver still will take place, and while the hippies may not succeed with their coup, they'll surely hurl Washington into chaos, playing hell with every aspect of domestic life, to say nothing of America's image abroad. So what we really want you to find out is precisely when and where the pollution maneuver is supposed to take place. Only if we catch the hippies red-handed as they're about to dump the LSD into the Potomac will we really foil the plot."

"That's quite a tall order."

He lifted his glass in toast. "And you're just the man who can handle it."

I started to protest, but he cut me off.

"Here's a phone number in Arlington, Virginia," he said, pulling a crumpled slip of paper from the pocket of his leather shirt. "It's registered in the name of one Matilda Damon. Ostensibly she's your dear maiden aunt, whom you call almost daily. Actually she's one of my subordinates, whose only job for the present will be to wait for

29

your messages and deliver them to me."

"Just what I always wanted," I observed. "A dear maiden aunt."

He ignore the comment. "And don't worry about running up a bill. I want to hear from you at least once a day—more often if the situation warrants it."

I memorized the number, then touched a match to the slip of paper and dropped it into an ashtray.

"Next," he went on, "you'll need some money." He pulled a roll of bills from his shirt and thrust them into my hands. "There's five hundred dollars here, all in tens and twenties. Be generous with your hippie friends, and they'll be more apt to talk to you. But, of course, don't be too generous. We don't want to arouse suspicion. If you use all this, ask Aunt Matilda for more. She'll send it to you posthaste. And, of course, keep her informed of any change of address. We'll want to be able to keep in touch with you at all times. You're not the only one of our people on this job, and some of the others have orders to keep an eye on you, just in case you get into trouble. But one never can tell what might go wrong."

"Like one's running afoul of nasty little men armed with strands of piano wire?"

"Among other possibilities, yes." He dug into his shirt again and produced a bottle of pills. "Next, here is some LSP. As you can see, it worked wonders with your sleeping princess. Perhaps you'll find it useful to become acceptable. Remember, if there's anything these hippies are really interested in, it's drugs. Show them a new kick and you'll make yourself a lot of friends in a hurry."

"The point is well taken."

"Next, get as close as you can to a fellow called The Big Head."

"You mean the high priest of The Church of the Sacred Acid?"

"Yes. Do you know him?"

30

"By reputation." I gestured toward Lola. "Sleeping beauty here thinks he's one of the foremost religious leaders of all time."

"Most of his followers agree with her. For my money, he's a nut. But so were Hitler and Mussolini. Anyway, he bears watching. All three of the bad-trip hippies interviewed at the public health clinics named him as the man behind the plan."

"You mean he's the mastermind?"

"Maybe. Or maybe he's just a figurehead. Whatever the case, he seems to be involved right up to his eyeballs. And since we don't have any other concrete leads, you might as well start with him."

"Finally"— he dipped into his shirt again—"here's a photograph. Study it carefully, then give it back to me."

I held it up to the light. It was a picture of a girl—lithe, long-limbed and luscious. Her long black hair toppled over her shoulders like an inky waterfall. Her eyes were sparkling brown, and her bright pink lips were parted in a sexy come-hither smile. She was wearing a topless go-go outfit that revealed the body of a doll who could have been in *Playboy*.

"Your wife?" I deadpanned.

"Corinne LaBelle," he replied dryly. "She's a biochemist."

"And the costume? Is this the latest thing in lab outfits?"

"The photo was taken when she was doing some undercover work for the agency as a go-go girl. It's the best picture we have of her."

"I don't doubt it."

"If you'll pay a little closer attention, you'll notice that she has a small, heart-shaped tattoo on her left breast.

"If you happen to run across her, you can use the tattoo as a positive means of identification."

"Does she usually run around with an exposed left breast?"

"Come now, my friend. A man with your talents shouldn't have trouble seeing her tattoo."

I took another look at the picture. The tattoo was there, all right. And the breast on which it was situated, along with the unmarked mammary which dangled deliciously nearby, made me suddenly very interested in the people who practice biochemistry. "You can rest assured that I'll explore the matter fully the first chance I get." I grinned. "Meanwhile, at the risk of sounding obtuse, might I ask how she's connected with the project at hand?"

"You might."

"All right, how's she connected with the project at hand?"

"A few years ago, Miss LaBelle was an assistant professor of biochemistry at a major university in France. However, her interest in politics eclipsed her interest in biochemistry, and she was dismissed for propagandizing her students with some of the most militant right-wing doctrines this side of Louis XIV. Still she remained committed to her ideology and presently began traveling throughout France as an itinerant rabble-rouser. Her physical charms persuaded many a Frenchman to heed her words, but, of course, memories of the Nazi occupation still were strong among other Frenchman and finally charges were sworn out against her. Whereupon she left the country without benefit of a passport and slipped into Canada, then into the United States. Here she took a job as a lab assistant with a pharmaceutical firm in Philadelphia and tried to shroud herself with the cloak of anonymity, presumably until the political climate in France changed enough to permit her safe return."

"But, of course, France's political climate never changed."

"Exactly. The rightists were defeated soundly in the subsequent election, and Miss LaBelle appeared doomed to spend the next four years, and perhaps longer, as a disgruntled exile. That's when we made her acquaintance."

"We? Meaning the agency?"

"Correct. We had learned about her from the immigration authorities, with whom we work very closely. We persuaded them not to prosecute her for illegal entry. Then we induced her to join our team."

"Failing which, she'd be deported?"

"I couldn't have put it better myself."

"You people really play all the angles."

"In this business, one has to. Anyway, we arranged for her to get a grant from the Thaddeus X. Coxe Foundation —a grant identical to the one you got for your Hamburg caper. We sent her on a mission in French Morocco, then another mission in the Sudan. These were followed by several missions in Africa, then her stint as a go-go girl in a San Francisco nightclub."

"What were you investigating there?"

"The possibility of communist influences among the student body at Berkeley." He chuckled. "Miss LaBelle produced quite a dossier."

"I wouldn't doubt it."

"Anyway, after San Francisco, we sent her to Hong Kong, where, under the pretense of investigating the nutritional value of certain varieties of seaweed found in Kowloon Harbor, she spied on the Chinese communists. She managed to gain the confidence of an extraordinary number of important sources, and her reports proved invaluable to us. Indeed, she was one of our most highly-prized agents."

"With assets like these"— I nodded toward her breasts —"it's no wonder."

"Yes. Anyway, we suddenly lost contact with her. There were no more reports, and our other people in Hong Kong couldn't find a trace of her. If she hadn't been so thoroughly committed to rightist ideologies, we might have suspected that she defected to the Reds. But, of course, the

33

circumstances under which we originally made contact with her negated that possibility. So we could only conclude that she had been discovered by the commies and murdered, or perhaps kidnapped. In any case, we never heard from her again. The last word we received was one of her reports about the Red Chinese plan to infiltrate the hippies."

"She was connected with that?"

"Not merely connected. She unearthed the whole thing singlehandedly."

I gave the picture another look and appreciated the reasons why many otherwise-loyal communists might have shared their deepest secrets with her.

"You really know how to dig up good agents."

"Thank you."

"But you still haven't told me how she fits in with my mission. Or are you just showing me the picture for esthetic reasons?"

"I'm showing you the picture," he replied, "on the remote chance that we've misgauged the firmness of her right-wing commitment—or on the less remote chance that the Chinese Reds have brainwashed her into joining their team. In either event, you may come across her in your travels."

"Tell me more."

"Well, as I mentioned earlier, she's a biochemist and the plot to pollute the Washington water supply is essentially a problem in biochemistry. LSD is an American discovery, and so far as we've been able to learn no communist country has produced it. It's not out of the question that the Reds might have kidnapped her and forced her to go to work for them."

"Still, it's unlikely that I'd run across her. After all, she could do anything she had to do in Peking as well as here. Would the communists, if they had kidnapped her, take the chance of letting her loose in America?"

34

"Presumably not. But that's just one more of the curious puzzles about this case. You see, we believe that she's presently here in New York."

"What makes you think so?"

"Two things. First of all, during her last three months in Hong Kong, she drew unusually large sums of money from her account with the Coxe foundation—all told, something like twenty thousand dollars. When questioned on it, she said that she needed the money to bribe her sources. We found this acceptable, and her reports were so valuable to us that we gave her all she asked for. Still, suspicious creatures that we are, we recorded the serial number of every bill we gave her. Lately, a great many of these bills have popped up at Federal Reserve banks in New York. Secondly, while in Philadelphia she had a boyfriend, an accountant named James Hartley. Last week Mr. Hartley abruptly walked off his job and moved to Manhattan. He presently resides in a sleazy rooming house on Twenty-Third Street."

"Very interesting," I quipped. "A no-account accountant."

Walrus-moustache took back the photo of Corinne and handed me one of a slender, boyish type with steel-rimmed glasses and a mole on his right cheek. "This is Hartley. The address of the rooming house is on the back of the picture. You'd be tipping our hand if you approached him directly, but memorize the address. You never can tell when it might come in handy."

"Done," I said.

He took back the photo, slipped it into his shirt and got up from the bed. "And that, Damon," he told me, "takes care of tonight's business. You know what we're after. Go get it. And"— he raised a warning finger —"don't smoke the grass or let it grow under your feet. As I said earlier, the hippies almost certainly have overcome the technical problems surrounding the pollution of the Potomac—or soon will. They can strike at any moment. Your country is counting on you to deliver the goods before they do." He straightened his leather shirt, hoisted his bermuda shorts, smoothed out his toupee, adjusted his Ben Franklin spectacles and tugged at the ends of his Walrus-moustache. "Now, as they say in the movies, I must be off. Ta-ta and all that."

I didn't bother to show him to the door. As far as I was concerned, he had found his way in, so he could find his way out. I waited until the click of the latch testified to his departure. Then I shucked my robe and returned to Lola.

Her smooth, succulent body wriggled awake as soon as I touched her. Her pretty blue eyes popped open, and a sexy smile lit up her face. "Baby," she purred. "I can still feel the tingles. What did you give me?"

"A pill," I replied, cupping one of her breasts in my hand.

"I'm still flying," she cried.

Her fingers found their way up my thigh. She quivered with delight at my readiness. She began to lick my body and then me. Slowly she scraped her teeth up and down and I held my breath. Would she bite it off? The scraping stopped and she licked it, then we joined normally.

Her long legs coiled around mine, and her fingernails dug into my back. "Oh, baby," she moaned. "We're going to make it and make it and make it. We're going to make it until you're so down you'll never come up again."

There was no harm in letting her try.

CHAPTER 3

It was six a.m. when Lola finally threw in the towel. Smiling weakly, though in ecstacy, she flopped over on one side of the bed and fell asleep. Since I couldn't do much to save the nation at that hour of the morning, I joined her.

When I woke up it was noon. The blazing New York sun had turned the apartment into a warm oven. Lola was in the kitchen, trying gamely to whip up a batch of scrambled eggs. I showed her how to do it. Then we breakfasted, and I made a date with her for eight that evening to take in one of The Big Head's sermons at The Church of the Sacred Acid. She promised that after the sermon she'd arrange for me to meet the great man personally. She mumbled something about moving in.

After she left, I showered, dressed and subwayed uptown to the Forty-Second Street branch of the public library. I was sure that there'd be something on The Big Head in their files of old magazines and newspapers, and I wanted to find out as much about him as I could.

What I found wasn't exactly an intimate biography, but when all the odds and ends were pieced together, a pretty clear picture emerged.

Color it kooky.

The Big Head's real name was Worthington Matthew McGee. According to *Time*, he was the scion of an old-line family of Ohio industrialists. According to *Newsweek*, he was the scion of an old-line family of Pennsylvania

37

industrialists. Whatever the case, both mags agreed that his parents had always had more loot than they knew what to do with. And they spent a sizable chunk of it putting him through school. He had prepped at Groton, taken his B.S. at Yale and picked up his Ph.D. in experimental psychology at the University of Pennsylvania.

During the Korean war, he had served as a lieutenant in the Army's Adjutant General Corps. Curiously, he had been discharged in 1952 while the war was still going full tilt and all discharges were supposedly frozen. No enterprising journalist had seen fit to look into this inconsistency, but it was safe to assume that the discharge had come under other-than-honorable conditions.

After the war, he went into research. His specialty was planarians, or flatworms. He published one monograph and two journal articles demonstrating that the slimy creatures could learn to work their way through a maze faster after being fed certain chemical compounds than they could without the compounds. The scientific community was quite impressed with his findings, and he was offered a professorship at a major university in the West.

He took the job, but he didn't keep it. Nor did he keep any of the others which followed it. Between 1955 and 1960, for reasons unexplained by any of the news accounts, he was on the faculty of no fewer than six different universities, each of lower academic standing than its predecessor. Finally he wound up at a nondescript teachers' college in Massachusetts.

It was in Massachusetts that he learned about the work being done with LSD by Drs. Timothy Leary and Richard Alpert at Harvard. He tried the drug himself, experimented with it on some students, got fired by the college, and in 1963 took to the road touting the glories of love.

As an itinerant love-touter, his career was nothing short of spectacular. He had preached in twenty-odd states and had been arrested in at least five of them on charges

38

ranging from "possession of marijuana" to "lewd and indecent behavior." Two of the arrests had resulted in convictions and were presently under appeal.

Meanwhile, between 1954 and 1962, he had been married and divorced four times, and none of his wives had stayed with him for longer than a year. Some batting average for a guy who roamed the country talking about love!

Tucking away the biographical sketch in my mental filing cabinet, I headed back to my apartment. I took another shower and changed into the East Village version of evening clothes—dark jeans and a long-sleeved shirt. I met Lola and treated her to dinner at one of the hippie restaurants and hailed a cab for The Church of the Sacred Acid. Tickets for two cost five bucks.

The so-called church was nothing more than a huge loft gone psychedelic. Strobe lights flashed madly back and forth across the ceiling. Movie projectors hurled bizarre images like copulating amoebas against the walls. The smoke of burning incense filled the air.

At one end of the room was an elevated platform surrounded by a black velvet curtain. When the audience was assembled on the wooden benches which served as pews, the house lights went out and the curtain opened, revealing a low wooden table—presumably the altar. It was painted white and stood in stark contrast to the black walls behind it. Except for a gleaming silver microphone stand, the rest of the platform was bare.

Suddenly four loudspeakers crackled to life. A low voice said, "Testing, one, two, three, four." Then, amidst murmurs of awe, a white-robed figure opened a door at the rear of the platform and stepped into the spotlight.

He carried a hand microphone and a small bouquet of roses. His robe reached the tops of his sandaled feet. Around his neck was a string studded with pointed ivory objects resembling oversized hound's teeth. His long, steel-

39

gray hair shot up from his head like a crop of wild grass, and his bright blue eyes glowed with the intensity of burning coals. Handing the flowers to a pretty brunette who sat at the edge of the platform, he went into his spiel.

"All right, man," he began, "you've got hang-ups. There's nothing wrong with that. Everybody's got hang-ups. But what're you gonna do about your hang-ups? That's the question.

"You tried booze, didn't you? You slopped up the old foam like a pig at a trough. But it didn't work, did it?

"So you tried downies. Tranquilizers. You took 'em three times a day, just like the doctor said. And that didn't work either, did it?"

"So now you're asking me.

"And I'm gonna tell you, baby.

"The answer is love.

"That's right, love.

"I say LOVE.

"Do you hear me?

"LOVE!!!"

Getting into the spirit of things, I draped my arm over Lola's shoulders and let my fingers come to rest on her breast. In reply, she brought her hand to my lap, but the gesture was perfunctory. Her real interests lay on the platform where the white-robed high priest of The Church of the Sacred Acid was spouting off like an updated Elmer Gantry.

"Are you listening to me?" he bellowed. "I'm talking about love.

"Do you know what it is?

"It's the morning and the evening star, that's what it is.

"It's not new. It's been around for a long, long time.

"But there isn't enough of it. There's never enough.

"Jesus had the answer.

"Buddha had the answer.

"Moses had the answer.

40

"They all had the answer.

"But nobody listened. The thieves and the hypocrites distorted their words and sold a bum bill of goods to the multitudes.

"Jesus said, 'Love.' He said, 'Love thy neighbor as thyself.'

"Then the phoney-baloneys in the black robes changed it. They said, 'Never mind your neighbor, baby. Go to church on Sunday and don't eat meat on Friday. That's where it's at.'

"Now you're asking me, 'Where's it really at?'

"And I'm telling you.

"It's in your head, baby.

"It's up there in your head, just waiting to come out."

I had my own ideas about where it was—and my head wasn't the place. I tried to get the message across to Lola by maneuvering her fingers into position around the pillar of my manhood. She clutched me dutifully, but she was too wrapped up in The Big Head's eloquence to put any feeling into the gesture.

"Yes, baby," he continued, "it's in your head.

"And I'm gonna tell you how to bring it out. All you gotta do is listen.

"Hello, Jesus. Say-hey, Moses. Good evening, your aggregate holiness, whatever your race, color or creed. Are you listening to me? I have some people here who want to know how to love. And I'm going to tell them.

"Are you listening, people?

"I want love.

"I want LOVE!

"I want the Ten Commandments—and not by Harvey and the Moonglows.

"I want the real Ten Commandments.

"LOVE! LOVE! LOVE! LOVE! LOVE! LOVE! LOVE! LOVE! LOVE! LOVE!"

The more he talked about it, the more I wanted it too.

41

But I wasn't getting it from Lola. Her eyes were riveted to The Big Head with the concentration of a hypnotic subject. With the first "LOVE" she loosened her grip on me. With the third she let go of me completely. And, by the time the tenth had rolled around, her hand had slithered off my thigh and was between her knees. So much for the Ten Commandments of Love!

Then suddenly another girl's hand found its way into my lap. It came from my left, the side opposite Lola, and headed straight for home plate. When it got there, it gripped me vigorously. The soft purr of appreciation that came from the throat of its owner let me know that she was delighted to find me in the state I was always in. I was glad we were off in a corner, back in the last—and empty—row.

I slid closer to her, feeling the soft firm flesh of her thigh against mine. I couldn't see her too clearly in the dim light of the darkened loft, but what I saw I liked.

Her long black hair toppled over her shoulders. Her pretty face was set in a feigned expression of rapt attention to the proceedings on stage. She wore a tight white sweater that displayed her small, round breasts to maximum advantage. And the bare legs that stretched out under her miniskirt were smooth, shapely and oh-so-caressable.

I reached around her and massaged the gentle curve where her left thigh met her belly. In response, she shifted her weight and eased her right thigh and buttock over my leg.

I moved farther to the left.

She moved farther to the right.

I moved still farther.

She moved still farther.

Then she was directly on top of me, her legs straddling mine, her fingers tugging desperately at the zipper.

My palms found the insides of her thighs and worked upward. She wore nothing underneath. In seconds I was exposed and she was wriggling to sit on my lap as we both

42

faced the rostrum. There was a moment's hesitation. Then she bore down and the throbbing engine steamed into port.

On stage, The Big Head was still mouthing off on the glories of love.

"Yes, baby," he was saying, "love is all you need, and I'm gonna tell you how to get it.

"You can't steal it.

"That twisting string of cash won't buy it, because cash is the curse of materialistic society.

"So how do you get it?

"I'll tell you how you get it.

"It's in your head, man. It's right up there in your head.

"And how does it come out?

"It comes out at night. It comes out at night because it's afraid. The cash-crazy world wants to buy and sell it and it doesn't want to be bought or sold.

"So it's afraid. Like, can you blame it, man? Wouldn't you be afraid?

"But it doesn't have to be afraid. We can make it unafraid.

"And how can we do that?

"By transforming the world, that's how.

"Yes, man, we've got to transform the world.

"We've got to stamp out hate and war and money. Then the world'll be ready for love.

"LOVE!

"That's what I'm telling you.

"LOVE!!

"Do you hear me?

"LOVE!!!"

Each time he said "LOVE" a ripple of rapport surged through the audience. My new-found friend expressed her empathy by squeezing tightly. I silently hoped The Big Head would say "Love," more often.

He did. In fact, he said it all of twenty times. With each repetition, the audience grew more inflamed. Soon a chorus

43

had begun to chant with him: "LOVE, LOVE, LOVE!" My partner's contractions kept time with the chanting. Her grip was so tight I thought my circulation was going to be cut off.

Deep inside me, a hot ball of excitement swirled to life. I thrust harder. My miniskirted mate struggled to keep up with me. Her buttocks churned furiously. Her breasts strained against my hands.

My excitement mounted. She turned her head around toward me and I found her lips with mine. She thrust her tongue between them. With one hand I cupped her breast. With the other I reached beneath her skirt and rubbed vigorously against the mound of Venus.

A moment passed.

Then another.

Then our bodies exploded.

When it was over, we stayed in position. I kissed her neck and savored the heady aroma of her perfume. She squeezed harder, eager to consume every last ounce of passion. I held her to me and continued kissing her until her body went limp in my arms.

On stage, The Big Head, with flawless timing, had climbed out of the love bag and into the peace bag. He was saying that money was the root of all evil and that people would have to purge themselves of materialistic desire before the world could know lasting peace. He advocated unilateral disarmament, abolishment of taxation and a welfare program whereunder every man, woman and child would have a guaranteed annual wage. He never got around to explaining how a disarmed nation could protect itself against aggression or how a society without taxation could operate a welfare program. But if the congregation was aware of his inconsistencies, they didn't let on.

I tuned out the lecture and turned back in on my partner. Evidently she had just discovered the one exception to the rule that whatever goes up must also come down. She was rocking back and forth.

My hands found her hips and tried to slow her down. Actually I was ready to play an encore, but I didn't want to press my luck. So far Lola hadn't taken her eyes off the stage long enough to notice that I was cuddling with another cutie. If she did notice, she might decide that I wasn't sufficiently interested in The Big Head's sermon to merit a personal introduction to him afterward. And if she refused to introduce us, I'd have blown the only real lead I had on The Big Freak-Out.

"Cool it," I whispered into my pretty sexmate's provocatively perfumed ear. "We're going to attract an audience."

She threw her head back over my shoulder and gnawed at my jaw. "Screw 'em," she murmured dreamily. She began jouncing around vigorously.

"But," I protested, "my girlfriend?"

"Tough," she replied, tonguing my neck with abandon. The tempo of her hip movements increased.

I could see that my rhetoric wasn't getting me anywhere. So I decided to let her have her way, hoping to get things over with as quickly as possible.

Leaning back on the bench, I arched my hips upward. The new angle put more zing into things. She gasped, and the soft, smooth spheres of her buttocks hammered furiously. Her fingers dug into my legs. Planting my feet against the bench in front of me, I thrust harder. She thrust back and fought to keep up with me.

Finally she couldn't take it any more. Her legs trembled, and her fingernails dug hungrily into my thighs. Then, with a mad burst of movement, she soared over the top. Clutching her by the hips, I slid her off my lap on the upswing. I zipped my fly, snuggled close to Lola, and tuned in again on The Big Head.

Somewhere along the line he had climbed out of the

45

peace bag and back into the love bag. His face was red with excitement, and his enormous blue eyes were threatening to pop out of his head.

"Now," he was shouting, "I'm going to show you the POWER of love!

"That's right, the POWER!

"And the GLORY!

"And you're gonna SEE it!

"Right HERE!

"Like I said, love is afraid. The cash-crazy world wants to buy and sell it, like toothpaste and scouring pads. But love doesn't want to be bought and sold. So it stays inside, 'cause it's afraid.

"Only here—here in this church—it isn't afraid anymore."

"It isn't afraid, because it knows that all of us are pure, all of us are good, all of us have purged ourselves of the filthy, decadent materialism that's corrupting the world.

"So it'll come out in this church, man, and it'll come out tonight.

"You watch and I'll show you."

He walked to the edge of the platform and reached for the girl to whom he earlier had given his bouquet of roses. She took his hand and climbed onto the platform with him.

She was a Latin type, with black hair and flashing eyes. Her skin was deep olive and her features were extremely delicate. She wore a white cotton blouse, open at the throat, and a pair of jeans that displayed her slim, shapely legs to excellent advantage.

"This is Chiquita," he announced. "She's a girl who's known poverty, a girl who's known suffering. And she's a girl who knows love. Watch now and you'll see it."

On cue she walked across the front of the platform. With each step she plucked a rose from the bouquet and tossed it into the audience. "Flowers," she said sweetly with a faint

46

Spanish accent. "Flowers mean love."

"You heard her," rasped The Big Head. "Flowers mean love, and Chiquita knows love. Now watch and she'll show you."

When she had tossed away her last flower she came back to the center of the platform and stood in front of the table. The Big Head put the microphone on its stand and began clapping his hands rhythmically. The audience picked up the beat.

"Love!" he chanted. "Love! Love! Love!"

For a moment Chiquita stood motionless. Her eyes were fixed on some point in the distance and her expression was blank. Then the audience took up The Big Head's chant. Slowly her lips began to quiver and she swayed from side to side.

"She's on, man!" The Big Head shouted enthusiastically. "She's really on! Now watch, and you'll see love!"

The tempo of the clapping and chanting accelerated. Chiquita's movements became more pronounced. Her breasts rose and fell. Her hips swung into a slow, undulating movement.

"Love, Chiquita!" commanded The Big Head. "Love! LOVE!"

Suddenly she dropped to her knees and ripped open her blouse. She wore nothing underneath, and her large, round breasts jutted out with a proudness that startled me.

The Big Head stood over her and scrutinized them. "Love!" he intoned. "These are the fruits of love! The full, firm fruits of love! Open your garden, Chiquita, and display the fruits of love! Love! LOVE!"

Her eyes were squeezed tightly shut. Her head was tossed back, and her long black hair cascaded wildly over her shoulders. The gleaming golden spheres of her breasts pulsated hotly in the bright white glow of the spotlight.

Slowly she removed her blouse completely, then un-

47

buttoned her jeans. The smooth lines of her belly came into view as she urged down the zipper and slid the waistband over her hips.

"Love!" prompted The Big Head. "Love, Chiquita! Love!"

Slacks at half-mast, she got up and made her way to the upstage side of the low, white table. Facing away from the audience, she sat on the table's edge and slid into a supine position. Her breasts rose majestically, like twin mountain peaks. Her face was screwed up in an expression of sublime ecstasy.

"Love!" rasped The Big Head. "Love! Love! Love!"

Chiquita writhed on the table as if she were in the throes of orgasm. Her breasts quivered, and her slim hips darted from side to side.

"And now," The Big Head whispered dramatically. "we'll show you love."

He moved to the upstage end of the table. Holding the microphone aloft like a torch, he positioned himself between his enraptured acolyte's outstretched thighs. Then with his free hand, he made a cross-like gesture of benediction over her undulating womanhood.

"Love!" he said.

Another gesture.

"Love!"

Another.

"LOVE!"

The loft was silent.

The Big Head's eyes stared glassily into space.

Beads of perspiration glistened on his forehead.

His fingers tugged at his robe, and suddenly the garment fell open.

He was wearing nothing underneath.

"LOVE!!!" he shouted.

I strained forward, expecting to witness the ravishment of Chiquita.

48

It never happened.

The white-robed high priest of The Church of the Sacred Acid, standing twixt the thighs of one of the sexiest creatures a man could hope to see, was as limp as a strand of overcooked spaghetti.

"LOVE!!!" he repeated. "LOVE!!! Love so sure, so confident, so absolutely certain of itself that it needs no physical expression! LOVE!!! LOVE!!!"

Immediately every light in the house went out. There was a murmur from the audience. Then the lights went on again. When they did. the curtain had closed around the platform and The Church of the Sacred Acid looked like exactly what it was—a dingy loft filled with weird-looking people. The audience started toward the exits.

Lola and I headed for the center aisle. In front of us, my miniskirted ex-sexmate was thumbing casually through a dog-eared copy of the evening's program. She was alone, and as she rounded the corner I got a good look at her. She looked even better in the light than she had in darkness. She also looked vaguely familiar, but I couldn't remember when I had seen her before or where.

Lola took my hand and cuddled against me. "Wasn't it marvelous?" she cooed.

"The greatest," I replied, thinking more of my bout with the doll in the miniskirt than of The Big Head's graphic lesson in non-contact love.

"Most people miss the point," she went on. "I mean, they think it's a joke or something. They can't understand how The Big Head can have Chiquita lying there naked in front of him and not want to ball her."

"Well," I pointed out, "his act doesn't exactly have a boffo finish. The impotence bit is sort of anticlimax. Or should I say *pre*climactic?"

"But that's it! Like he said, his love is so great that it doesn't require physical expression! He can dig Chiquita without balling her, because he really knows where love's

49

at! The squares don't understand. But once you know what's happening, it's as clear as day."

It wasn't all that clear to me, but I didn't argue with her. I had other things on my mind—like the babe in the miniskirt. The more I looked at her, the more certain I was that I had seen her before. But where? And when? I thought hard, but couldn't make the connection.

The crowd in the aisle had thinned. Miniskirt had wiggled her way through three couples and was slithering out the door. I thought of asking Lola if she knew her. Then, in the interests of tact, I decided against it. We angled our way through a mob of longhairs at one of the exits and started down the stairs.

"Well," said Lola once we were outside, "are you ready for the party?"

I did a mild double-take. "What party?"

"You know! The party! Where I'm going to introduce you to The Big Head!"

"Oh, that party!" I pressed her hand with all the loving tenderness of a hunter patting his bloodhound on the head. "Lead the way, sugar. I can't wait to get there."

CHAPTER 4

The party was on Avenue D in a fourth-floor walk-up that was so decrepit it made my apartment look like the Presidential Suite at the New York Hilton. The guests were a couple of dozen hippies who were milling around regaling each other with tales of LSD trips. According to Lola, a swinging time was being had by all. I could imagine myself having more fun at a convention of the Daughters of the American Revolution. Or the Daughters of Sappho, for that matter.

The Big Head hadn't yet made the scene, so Lola introduced me to a few minor celebrities. There was a poet who was published regularly in *The East Village Other*, a sculptor whose works had graced the lobby of the Hotel Chelsea and a painter who took credit for oné of the abstract oils of Max's Kansas City. Each in turn told me how LSD had been responsible for his success and how he hoped to achieve even greater heights once he had taken a few more trips.

Next I met a pimply-faced creep named Egbert, who Lola identified as her employer. He was the leader of a rock and roll band called The Decline of the West. Originally they had been known as Marquis and the Sodomites, but the name had been scrapped because it conveyed an anti-love image. Next they had called themselves Niccolo and the Macchiavellians, but that had been dropped because it was too materialistic. Finally they

51

settled on The Decline of the West, which Egbert deemed not only loving and unmaterialistic but also symbolic—although symbolic of what he was at a loss to say. The name stuck.

Lola was The Decline of the West's hummer. Egbert had been standing on the corner of St. Mark's Place and Second Avenue one afternoon when she sauntered by humming a few bars of "A Whiter Shade of Pale." He had asked her if she wanted to hum professionally, and she had said yes. Now she and The Decline of the West were gigging around East Village on weekends and waiting for the big break that would, with the help of LSD, put them way up on top, along with Procol Harum, Bob Dylan, The Jefferson Airplane and The Moby Grape.

While Egbert spelled out his plans for the rise of The Decline of the West, I listened with one ear. With the other I tuned in on the conversations of the hippies around us. I was hoping to hear something, anything, that would tie in with The Big Freak-Out. But all I heard were paeans of praise for LSD.

One thing was certain: these acid-heads really dug their acid.

But were they plotting to take over the country? If they were, they weren't talking about it.

Finally, shortly after midnight, The Big Head arrived. He had traded in his white robe and sandals for a pair of orange plaid pants, a chartreuse shirt and a pair of tennis shoes. Around his neck was the string of hound's teeth he had worn during his sermon. On his arm, looking sexier than ever, was Chiquita.

My eyes took a quick tour of her sumptuous body. She was wearing a tight pink turtleneck and even tighter white slacks. I could see through the turtleneck that she hadn't bothered to put on a bra. I wondered if she also went lingerie-less south of the border, and I vowed to find out at the earliest possible moment.

52

The Big Head and his pretty tail wandered through the crowd exchanging pleasantries with the plebeians. I nudged Lola and we edged toward him. She caught his eye, gave him a big smile and asked him to meet Rod Damon. His face came alive with recognition at the mention of the name.

"Damon?" he repeated, giving me a firm handshake. "From the League for Sexual Dynamics?"

"One and the same."

"I've read your books. You've got quite a thing going for you." To Chiquita he explained, "He's a sex researcher, honey. Like Kinsey and those people. But he gives his work the personal touch. I'll bet he's balled more chicks in the last year than most men do in a lifetime."

Chiquita eyed me with interest. Lola suddenly became very interested also. "No wonder he's so great in bed!" she soliloquized. "I never dreamed I was making it with a certified expert."

The Big Head smiled. "He's certified, all right. And the money boys at the big foundations know it. What's that line from the magazine ads, Damon? While you're up, get me a grant?"

"He's always up," contributed Lola.

"'Up'?" echoed Chiquita. "What is 'up'? And what are 'grants'? And who are these 'money boys'? This language is very confusing to me."

"I'll explain later," said The Big Head. He turned back to me. "What brings you to East Village, Damon? Did you con somebody into subsidizing an investigation of the sexual mores of hippies? Or is this a busman's holiday?"

"I'm subsidized."

"Very neat. Nothing like mixing business with pleasure."

I grinned. "You should know."

"If that's a joke, sorry-but-I-don't-get-it."

My grin hardened. "Lola and I caught your act

53

tonight—at two-and-a-half bucks a head. There were all of a hundred people in the audience. Not a bad day's pay for a guy who thinks cash is the greatest evil this side of leprosy."

Lola squirmed, obviously embarrassed that I had addressed her idol in tones somewhat less than worshipful. But The Big Head took the dig in stride. "Well, I've got to make my bail money some way. But I'm no hypocrite, Damon. I believe in what I preach." His eyes took on something of the fervent glow they had radiated on stage earlier in the evening. "The world is going to hell in a handbasket. Look around you. Dehumanization is the password, and the fat cats on Wall Street are calling the tune. Kids are trained from birth to become cogs in the machinery of big business, if they don't wind up as cannon fodder first. Meanwhile, art is dying and literature is dead. There's only one hope for civilization. We've got to get back to the basics—love, humanity and brotherhood."

"In essence, you're not saying anything that Horace didn't say two thousand years ago."

"True. And Hesiod said it five hundred years before him. If you feel like adding to the list, you can ring in Mohammed, Christ, Luther, Thomas Acquinas, Dante, Goethe and Pope John XXIII. But what I have that they didn't is the pharmaceutical wonder called lysergic acid diethylamide, or LSD. When you use it, you wake up to the real beauties of the world, the beauties that materialistic society has managed to obscure. In the words of Tim Leary, you turn on, tune in and drop out. Or more elaborately stated, you experience a reorganization of your sensory faculties, you see things for what they really are, and you turn your back on the cash-crazy society that thinks happiness is nothing more than color TV sets, American Express credit cards and two cars in every garage."

Without realizing it, he had given me the opening I was

looking for. I jumped in feet first. "I'm all for acid," I told him. "I use it, and I think it's the greatest thing since indoor plumbing." He regarded me with an expression of new-found camaraderie. "But," I went on quickly, "I'm not against material conveniences. I happen to like color TV sets, American Express credit cards and two cars in my garage."

He smiled the smile of a true missionary all set to pounce upon a convert. "Our points of view aren't as incompatible as they may seem. I'm not against conveniences. I'm just opposed to the way society overemphasizes their importance."

I smiled back, the smile of the spider enticing the fly into its lair. "Then maybe we're on the same side after all. But our methods differ. You take the long-range view. You're preaching to a handful of kids and hoping that two or three generations from now they'll have carried your message throughout the world. Me—I'm not so patient. I want things to happen while I'm still young enough to get in on the action."

His eyes narrowed. "What sort of things?"

I lowered my voice conspiratorially. "I've got a few ideas. But this isn't the time or place to discuss them. If you're really interested, why don't we get together some afternoon for lunch?"

For a moment he said nothing. I could visualize the wheels inside his brain spinning around. I made a little bet with myself. If he had nothing to do with The Big Freak-Out, he'd dismiss me with a cordial don't-call-me-I'll-call-you. On the other hand, if he was as involved as Walrus-moustache seemed to think, he'd be bursting with curiosity and he'd want to pow-wow with me as soon as possible.

I waited for his reply.

"Well," he said finally, "I'm not doing anything tomorrow afternoon. How about you?"

"My schedule's wide open."

"Two o'clock too early for you?"

"Just right."

"Where should we meet?"

"How about Max's Kansas City?"

"Fine."

There wasn't anything more for either of us to say. We shook hands, exchanged nice-meeting-you's and drifted off in opposite directions. I waited until he was out of range, then permitted myself a big cat-that-ate-the-canary grin. So The Big Head wanted to hear my ideas. Eight to five he was now second-guessing me twice as hard as I had been second-guessing him. And unless I missed my bet, he'd be second-guessing me right up to the time of our lunch date. Now to figure out some ideas to put an end to his second-guessing, and at the same time lure him into selling me on joining in on The Big Freak-Out!

But that could wait until morning. Meanwhile, I still had Lola on my hands, along with a roomful of hippies. For The Big Head's benefit, I'd have to pretend I was enjoying the party as much as he was.

I steered Lola back toward a corner of the room where Egbert and two other members of The Decline of the West were holding forth on the powers and glories of acid. The five of us chatted about music and acid, love and acid, East Village and acid, and acid and acid. Then we went through the whole routine again. It was the sort of conversation that'd give anyone but a dyed-in-the-wool hippie a terminal case of yawns. But I stifled mine. I had an image to project, and the fate of the world was hanging on how well I projected it.

Fifteen minutes passed, then fifteen more. Someone had turned on a record player and a few couples were dancing. Others were clustered in small groups, passing around thin, hand-rolled cigarettes that had to be marijuana. I noticed that Lola and her chums weren't indulging, and I asked her

56

why. "We're cooling it till it's time for the good stuff," she replied. I didn't quite follow her, but I pretended I did. Nothing destroys an image like an admission of ignorance.

Another fifteen minutes passed, then another. The crowd began to thin. Soon it was three a.m. and the number of partyers had shrunk to the original two dozen that had been there when we arrived. Then it was four a.m. and the crowd numbered no more than twelve or thirteen.

Finally, at four thirty, a longhair-type wearing blue jeans and a psychedelic sportshirt locked the door. The record player promptly went off, and the crowd gathered around The Big Head, who was standing alongside a table with a bottle of pills in his hand. I slipped into place next to him.

"Acid?" I asked, nodding toward the bottle.

He nodded back. "Want to turn on with us?"

I produced the bottle of LSP capsules that Walrus-moustache had given me the night before. "Let me turn *you* on," I said. "I'm in a loving mood, and there's more where these came from."

He took the bottle from me, held it up to the light and whistled under his breath. "Am I seeing things, or is this The Big P?"

I didn't know what he meant, but I had a good idea we were on the same wavelength. "LSP," I replied, covering myself both ways. "You've heard of it, of course."

"Sure. I've got a few mikes of it at my pad. But not enough to play Santa Claus with. In New York it's harder to find than female roosters. Where'd you connect?"

I flashed a hippier-than-thou smile. "One of my buddies at the university whipped up a batch. I don't mind sharing the wealth."

He gave me a look that was one part doubt and one part grudging admiration. Then, evidently, he put aside the doubt. "Fellow lovers," he announced to the hippies, "our buddy Damon has just volunteered to turn us on with the hottest new drug this side of dreamland—LSP. If you want

57

in, hold out your hand. If not, help yourself to the old standby." He put his bottle of LSD on the table for the standbyers.

Lola snuggled up alongside me, beaming with pride at having introduced me to the obviously admiration-filled hippies. The Big Head uncapped my bottle and began passing out the capsules to the longhairs who had rapidly queued up in front of him. Adventurous to a fault, every last cat and chick in the crowd has eschewed the LSD for the new stuff.

When everyone had a pill, The Big Head gave me back my bottle. I took one for myself and one for Lola. Then I waited for Our Leader to lead the way.

"Here's to Damon," he said, hoisting the capsule in a gesture of toasting. "May he live as long as he wants to, and may he want to as long as he lives."

"To Damon," echoed the hippies. Then, following their leader's lead, they popped the pills into their mouths and swallowed hard.

I was tempted to palm mine and merely pretend that I had swallowed it. But I didn't dare take the chance. The Big Head was watching me. I wasn't sure that I'd be able to simulate an acid high successfully, and if I failed the jig would be up. So, putting duty before personal preference, I joined the crowd. Then I waited for the stuff to jolt me into hallucinogenville.

I didn't have to wait long. The pill had barely gone down my throat before I began to sway dizzily. Then a weird sensation of weightlessness overtook me, and the next thing I knew I was floating toward the ceiling, belly-up.

"Hey!" I yelled. "Get me down from here! You over there! Somebody! Anybody! Get me down!"

I saw Egbert run up the side of the wall and walk upside down toward me. He smiled, patted me lightly on the head and walked away.

I walked along the ceiling after him, then down the wall

58

and back onto the floor. For a moment things seemed normal enough, and I congratulated myself on having regained my mental equilibrium. Then the room started spinning wildly, and I clutched the first thing in sight to steady myself.

What I had clutched was Chiquita's breasts. They were right in front of me, thrusting out of her turtleneck like a pair of twin melons. They felt good in my hands, but then suddenly they started growing bigger. Soon they were the size of two huge beach balls. I struggled to keep my grip on them, lost and fell to the floor.

The room stopped spinning, and things seemed normal again. I inched my way toward the corner and sat in it. Then I closed my eyes and tried to act as inconspicuously as possible.

But closing my eyes hadn't been such a good idea. No sooner had my lids come down than I started seeing the wildest things imaginable.

First there were colors—raw, naked colors, of the most fantastic shades and hues I had ever seen. They gushed through the room like torrents of water, overpowering everything in their wake.

Then came the animals. Elephants, tigers, rats and giant ants. I tried to run away from them, but everywhere I turned they came after me. Finally a huge walrus came between me and them, and with one stroke of his whip, killed them all. What a relief!

Then I felt weightless again—as light as air and twice as billowy. It was calm and nice. Very nice. Then I heard music. And I saw it. Yes, I actually saw it floating through the air, just as I was floating. It was all very peaceful.

Until the walls started breathing.

I didn't really mind that they were breathing. Like, why should I care what they did?

But they were breathing so damned loud they ruined it for the rest of us!

59

I walked over to one of them and told it to quiet down.

It wouldn't listen.

I tried to reason with it.

No dice.

Finally I resorted to violence. I took a bottle of club soda and flung it right between the wall's eyes. That did it. I didn't hear another sound from the walls for the rest of the night.

It wouldn't have mattered even if I had, because by then I was too tired to care. All I wanted to do was sleep. I went back to the corner where I had seen the music and I closed my eyes. The colors came at me again, but this time they were softer and more peaceful. They wrapped themselves around me like billowy clouds and we went to sleep together.

When I woke up I was looking into the eyes of a woman.

A beautiful woman.

She was lithe, long-limbed and luscious. Her long black hair toppled over her shoulders like an inky waterfall. Her eyes were sparkling brown, and her bright pink lips were parted in a sexy come-hither smile.

I tried to remember where I had seen her before, but I couldn't. Then suddenly I did remember. I had seen her on a photograph—a snapshot which showed her wearing a topless go-go outfit.

"Your wife?" I heard myself asking Walrus-moustache.

"Corinne LaBelle," his voice replied. "She's a biochemist. If you'll pay a little closer attention, you'll notice that she has a small, heart-shaped tattoo on her left breast. See it there next to the nipple?"

I looked, but I saw nothing. Her nipple—along with the rest of her breast—was covered by a smartly tailored dress.

"Come now, my friend," the voice continued. "A man with your seductive talents shouldn't have any trouble persuading her to expose it."

60

I reached for the buttons on her dress, but she backed away.

"Wait!" I said.

But she wouldn't. As I struggled to reach her, she slid out of my grasp, scampering across the room and out the door.

I tried to get up and follow her, but my body was glued to the floor. She vanished and I closed my eyes and went back to sleep.

The next thing I knew I was huddled in a corner of the kitchen with Egbert, the leader of The Decline of the West. "Damon," he was saying, "this country's in bad shape. What we need is a total change of direction, a return to the peaceable ways of our ancestors. And we can't get it by operating within the system. We have to take radical action, forceable action. In short, we need a revolution."

"Agreed," I replied. "But how do we pull it off?"

He smiled. "You've heard of flower power, haven't you?"

"Sure."

"What does it mean to you?"

"Everybody loves everybody else and proves it by giving them flowers."

He let loose with a macabre Bella Lugosi laugh. "That's what we've convinced the public. But the real flower power is something quite different. It's militant. It goes straight for the jugular. And it gets the enemy with their own weapon—force."

"I don't follow you."

"Then listen closely. What would you say if I told you that right now there are several hundred hippies all set to overthrow the government?"

"I'd ask you how you plan to do it."

"With LSD, Damon. With LSD."

"I still don't follow you."

"Well, what would you say if I told you that we plan to pollute the water supply of Washington, D.C., with enough acid to turn on the whole city? And that when everybody is turned on we plan to . . . zdvlhas;ohepowe;bdlkbdbdk-bweb?"

I gulped and tried to clear my head. He still was talking, but I wasn't receiving him. Colors were flashing through my brain and the room was spinning wildly. I grabbed his shoulder for support. "Wait!" I said. "Give it to me again after the part where everybody is turned on."

He patted me on the head. "It's kind of hard to understand, but try, because you'll be glad you did. Now, like I was saying, there'll be half a dozen platoons hiding out in unobtrusive apartments throughout Washington and its suburbs. The headquarters will be in Chevy Chase, Maryland . . . zvs½0hd;h5hf;oihc;ohandflkjdhad and they'll all be armed to the teeth. Vsgdhgff;kjh;khdhfjhfkjh-fjhg . . ."

"*Wait!*" I screamed. The colors had become brighter, and the room was spinning even faster. My legs were getting wobbly, and it took all the energy I could summon to keep on my feet.

He looked at me sympathetically, as if to say he understood my difficulty in keeping up with him.

"Go back to the Chevy Chase part," I said. "Give—it—to—me—again—"

He tried, but it was useless. No sooner would he get three or four words out than my mind would wander and I'd have to ask for a replay. Finally I couldn't even ask anymore. My words had become as incomprehensible as his.

He gave me another pat on the head. "Don't sweat it, baby," he smiled. "There's plenty of time." Then he ambled out of the kitchen. I tried to follow him, but my knees buckled and my body went slack. I wound up in an unconscious heap on the floor.

When I came to, I was standing in my old corner of the living room and Lola was kneeling in front of me. She was naked, and her hands were tugging frantically at my belt. I tried to help her unloosen it, but my arms hung at my sides like a pair of lead weights. Finally she abandoned the attempt and unzipped my fly. Then, reaching inside, she pulled out her friend.

"Oh, baby!" she told it. "I thought I'd never see you again! Why don't you write or something?"

The way things had been going all night, I wouldn't have been surprised if she got an answer. But she didn't wait for one. Clutching the base of the shaft with eager fingers, she took the tip in her mouth and began making slow, warm circles around it with her tongue.

I was filled with desire—but not only for Lola. My eyes had drifted across the room, where Chiquita and two other girls were sitting on a couch. All three were naked, and I was lusting after them like I had never lusted after anyone before.

"Come here!" I called to them. When they ignored me, I repeated, "Come here!"

To my surprise, all three of them got up from the couch and crossed the room toward me.

I clutched Lola by the hair and tried to tear her away from me. She looked up, and her eyes were full of fire.

"Later," I snapped.

"Later," she mumbled. Her legs twisted around mine like two snakes climbing a tree, and her tongue slithered gently up and down the instrument of my passion.

"Help," I cried weakly.

I looked down at Lola. She was clutching me more tightly than ever, and her tongue was swirling back and forth across my overheated loveshaft. Nothing impeded her progress this time, because all my clothes had mysteriously vanished and I stood there as naked as everyone else.

"Help," I repeated softly, "or join in."

63

The cutie on Chiquita's left, a tall redhead with breasts the size of volleyballs, leaned toward me. I grabbed her splendid spheres and gyrated them in frantic circles. In reply, she leaned closer still. Her mouth found mine, and our tongues locked.

Meanwhile, the brunette on Chiquita's right had crept around me. Her deft fingers had taken firm hold of my buttocks, and her tongue went wild.

Chiquita surveyed the proceedings like a general surveying his troops. "All together now," she smiled, "a-one an' a-two an' a-three an' a-four."

"Turn on the bubble machine!" called The Big Head, suddenly materializing from nowhere. Having said his piece, he just as suddenly dematerialized.

The ministrations of my three nude démoiselles were beginning to take their toll. Inside me a volcano of passion was bubbling to life. I didn't want it to erupt—at least not until I had ditched the three second-stringers and paired off with Chiquita. She was the key to The Big Head.

"Come on, Chiquie," I said. "Help me get rid of these girls and we'll fly together."

To my happy astonishment, she obeyed. Clutching Lola by the shoulders, she turned her out of the saddle and sent her sprawling across the room. Then she beat away the redhead and the brunette, and finally we were alone together.

She lay on her back on the floor.

Her thighs parted to receive me.

I knelt between them—kissed her squarely and deliberately.

The hot, quivering lips of her womanhood wrapped lovingly around me.

All of a sudden, it was New Year's Eve, Halloween and the Fourth of July.

Fireworks exploded and colors flashed through my brain. Music danced in front of my eyes. Tantalizing fingers of sensation crawled up and down my legs. Then I moved up and she let me in.

I didn't know where the fireworks, the colors and the music were coming from. But there was no doubt about the source of the tantalizing fingers of sensation. Lola, the redhead and the brunette, finding that I had shelved them in favor of Chiquita, had decided not to be sore losers. All three of them had climbed on top of me, and their lips and tongues were grazing every exposed surface of my body.

Chiquita squirmed maddeningly beneath me. I pumped against her, harder and harder, faster and faster. The boiling lava inside me began rising to the surface.

Lola and her chums continued to work me over.

Chiquita continued to squirm.

The boiling lava continued to rise.

Then the whole world seemed to shake as the explosion coursed through me. I gasped, and abandoned myself to the most exquisite sensations I had ever experienced.

"*Ite, missa est*," intoned The Big Head, suddenly popping up alongside the bizarre tableau which our five bodies composed.

"You better believe it," replied Chiquita, sliding out from on bottom.

Then, before I realized what was happening, everyone had gone and I was all alone.

But not for long.

A few seconds after they had left, they all were back, this time with Corinne LaBelle among them. She stood to one side with The Big Head as I replayed the same foursome scene with the redhead as my prime object of assault.

The redhead was followed by the brunette, and the brunette was followed by Lola. Each time, everything happened the same way and the sensations were always unbelievable. I began to feel like an actor in a repertory company who plays the same role opposite a different

65

leading lady each night. It was a nice feeling. Then, quite suddenly, it stopped. Actually I stopped. If I kept it up I could kill myself. I passed out.

When the lights went on again, Lola and I were sitting together. Chiquita and one of the guys from The Decline of the West were sprawled across the couch on the other side of the room. Several other naked couples occupied places on the floor, and one imaginative twosome was locked around the legs of the table. The Big Head, fully clothed, was sitting alone with his back to the door. His arms were wrapped around his chest, his lips were blue and his body was trembling.

I rubbed my eyes and waited for a new round of hallucinations to start.

None did.

I stretched and took another look around the room.

Everything—and everyone—remained in place.

I listened for music.

There was none.

I stretched again and breathed a sight of relief. The effects of the drug had worn off.

Gingerly disengaging Lola's hand from its resting place, I stumbled to my feet. Every muscle in my body ached, and a dull pain was gnawing at the base of my skull. My throat was dry. My stomach felt as though someone had scrubbed it out with a steel wool pad.

I found my clothes and put them on. Then, helping myself to a can of beer from the refrigerator in the kitchen, I tried to sort out my thoughts.

It wasn't easy.

Obviously I had done a lot of hallucinating during the course of the night.

But just as obviously, I hadn't imagined *everything* I remembered.

The sex-play, for instance.

When I took the LSP, I had been fully clothed and so

66

had everyone else in the room. When its effects wore off, I was naked and so was everyone else—except The Big Head. This, plus the fact that my manhood was as sore as an exposed nerve ending, was pretty convincing evidence that I'd had more than my usual quota of sack-action.

But had I really played round-robin with four different chicks? Or had I just swung with Lola four times and hallucinated the rest.

And what about Egbert? Had he really started to give me a run-down on the plans for The Big Freak-Out? Or had I hallucinated that too?

And what about Corinne LaBelle? Had she actually been in the room?

I could only guess. And in the shape I was in, even guessing required more effort than I had energy for.

I polished off the beer, then stepped over a couple lying in the kitchen doorway and made my way back to the living room. Everything was exactly as I had left it, except that The Big Head, previously stone-silent, was now mumbling a weird litany of nonsense syllables. I squatted down alongside him. "What's happening, baby?" I asked.

His head jerked up and he looked at me through glassy eyes. "Shhhh," he said after a moment. "They'll hear you."

"Who?" I asked.

He drew his arms more tightly around his chest. His forehead was studded with beads of perspiration and his lips were quivering violently. "Them," he replied. "Who else?"

I played the game with him. "Can you see them?"

He looked around as if he were really trying to. Then he stared straight ahead. All of fifteen seconds passed before he turned to me again. When he did, he wore a look of astonishment, as if he had just noticed me for the first time.

"Well," I pressed, "can you see them or not?"

He took another look. "No," he said quietly. "But don't make any noise. They're around here somewhere."

I said nothing. A minute passed, then another, then a third. He was frozen in place, his lips trembling, his body curled up into a fearful-looking foetal ball. I waited a few minutes more, then said, "I don't hear them now. I think they're gone."

He looked around the room again, then turned back to me. "Do you really think so?"

"I'm sure of it. Otherwise we'd hear them, wouldn't we?"

"Yeah, we would."

Several more minutes passed, and he seemed to relax. He stretched out his legs and straightened his back against the door. "Wow, man!" he said, yawning. "What a trip!"

"A good one or a bad one?"

"A little of both." He chuckled. "But when it was good, it was very, very good."

"And when it was bad it was horrid," I finished the nursery rhyme for him.

Several more minutes passed. He blinked and massaged his temples. "Some stuff you handed out. I'd like to get more of it."

"I'll lay some on you tomorrow."

"Thanks."

"You're welcome."

Several more minutes. I decided to see if he could shed any light on my vision of Corinne LaBelle. "That brunette you were with," I said. "The one who didn't take her clothes off—who was she?"

He slid forward on the floor until he was in a supine position with only his head propped up against the door. "Just a chick, man. Just another chick."

I slid into place alongside him. "She had a lot going for her."

He yawned. "Ahhh, she was just a chick."

"Why didn't she take her clothes off?"

He turned toward me and his eyes fixed on mine. He

68

seemed to be looking at me from across a great distance. "Ahhh—" he began. Then, sliding down farther on the floor, he rolled onto his side, facing away from me. A few seconds later, he began to snore.

I headed back to the kitchen for another beer. I considered trying again to get some information out of him, then decided against it. In the shape he was in, he couldn't tell me much. And even if he could, he wouldn't, so there was no point pressing my luck.

I sipped the beer, trying to make some sense out of the little he *had* told me. One thing seemed certain: there had been a brunette in the room, a brunette who looked like Corinne LaBelle and who didn't take off her clothes. But was she really Corinne? And if she was, what was she doing at the party? Walrus-moustache seemed to think that she might have been kidnapped or brainwashed into serving the conspiracy. But in either case, would she have been socializing with the acid-heads? It didn't figure.

I looked out the window. The sun was coming up over the East River. A glance at my watch told me that it was six thirty. My aching bones told me it was time to go home and get some sleep.

I finished the beer and ambled back into the living room. Lola was still sitting in the corner, her face still frozen in an expression of ecstasy. I thought of waking her up, then changed my mind. I had enough problems without taking on the additional burden of playing nursemaid to a freaked out acid-head—especially a freaked out acid-head who, by introducing me to The Big Head had served her only purpose in my present scheme of things.

On the chance that Corinne LaBelle might still be on the premises, I made a quick inspection tour of all the girls in the apartment. None of them looked even vaguely like her. I slipped through the door and down the stairs.

Out on the street, the non-hippie citizens of the East Village—the Slavs, the Negroes and the Puerto Ricans

69

whose poverty and/or stubbornness had kept them chained to the neighborhood that rapidly was becoming a hippie preserve—were going about the business of beginning another day. Bleary-eyed men in working clothes and women in baggy dresses came tumbling out of apartment buildings. They queued up at the bus stops and subway kiosks, their faces portraits of patient despair.

I walked up Avenue D to the corner of Eighth Street, bought a newspaper and started the trek westward to my pad. I didn't glance at the headline until I was in my bedroom and half undressed. Then, when I did, I was too whacked out to really understand what I was reading.

I yawned, dropped the paper on the nighttable, took off the rest of my clothes and crawled into bed. Then I closed my eyes. They had been closed for all of a minute before the message hit me and I leaped out of bed like a cat with its tail on fire. I reread the headline.

"GARROTE MURDER

NUMBER FOUR

IN EAST VILLAGE"

A photograph of a familiar face stared out at me. The name under the picture was that of James Hartley, Corinne LaBelle's accountant-boyfriend from Philadelphia who had surfaced in New York a few days after she had dropped out of sight in Hong Kong. The caption under the picture was straight and to the point. It read, "VICTIM."

Hartley's corpse had been found in Tompkins Square Park at eleven the previous evening. Death was the result of strangulation with a strand of piano wire. Police knew only his name, his Twenty-Third Street address and—thanks to the fact that he carried a Pennsylvania driver's license—his previous address in Philadelphia. They had no theory as to who might have murdered him or why, but they suspected that his death was connected to the deaths of the three other hippies who had been garroted in the East Village during the past few weeks.

A reasonable suspicion, I mused, dropping the newspaper back onto the nighttable and flopping back into bed. Normally I might have thought about the murder longer. But my LSP trip had taken its toll. I was out cold as soon as my head hit the pillow.

CHAPTER 5

Sometimes it goes good and sometimes it goes bad. So far it had been going pretty good. During the first twenty-four hours after Walrus-moustache had tapped me to foil The Big Freak-Out, I had:

(1) Wangled an introduction to the plot's prime suspect without even leaving my apartment;

(2) Set up a luncheon date to pump him for information;

(3) Pow-wowed with a rock and roll musician who, unless I had been hallucinating, knew not only the general plan for the proposed coup but also the exact deployment of the troops who would stage it;

And (4)—again, unless I had been hallucinating—spotted the former U. S. secret agent who seemed to be either the prisoner or the reluctant collaborator of the conspirators.

Now, according to the law of averages, it was time for things to go bad.

The law was upheld.

Bad Break Number One came at Max's Kansas City, where I had my luncheon date with The Big Head. I got there at one forty-five, fifteen minutes ahead of schedule. An hour later, he still hadn't shown up. At three I began to get fidgety, and by three thirty I had decided to eat alone. I finished eating at four fifteen and he still was nowhere in sight. Then I polished off two beers. Soon it was five thirty

72

and the dinner crowd had started to make the scene. I had another beer and headed home. It was six o'clock, and The Big Head had stood me up but good.

I tried not to be too disappointed. I told myself that he probably was hung over from his LSP trip and that he'd be all smiles and apologies when I looked him up that evening at The Church of the Sacred Acid.

I was wrong. I got to The Church at seven, an hour before the sermon was supposed to begin, and found him not only unsmiling and unapologetic but also indisposed. The longhaired flunky who carried my message backstage returned with word that the great man was too busy to see me, either before the show or after. That was Bad Break Number Two.

I still didn't give up. I knew that hippies never placed a premium on politeness, and since The Big Head was the hippiest hippie of them all, it was only logical that he'd be somewhat lacking in the social amenities department. I decided to pay him another visit the following night. Then I chased down my second lead—Egbert, of The Decline of the West.

I found him at a sleazy coffeehouse called The Ink Well, where The Decline of the West was playing a midweek one-night stand. I suffered through an hour of the band's so-called music. Then, during the intermission I buttonholed their maestro and tried to get him to resume the conversation I remembered having with him at the party.

Bad Break Number Three—he seemed completely unaware that the conversation had taken place. When I tried to prod his memory by speaking of the need for a revolution which would turn the United States back toward the peaceable ways of our ancestors, he looked at me as if I had popped my cork. When I described flower power as a militant movement that aims to get the enemy with its own weapon, he told me that I was reading the wrong magazines and suggested that I try *Time*.

73

Finally I took a shot in the dark. I told him that I was part of an organization which planned to overthrow the United States government by polluting the Potomac with LSD, and I asked him to join in on the plot. He let me spell out all the details of the plan, then smiled at me like a kindergarten teacher refusing the request of a well-meaning but hopelessly dimwitted five-year-old. "It's a wild idea, Damon," he said, his voice loud and emphatic. "But it'll never work. If I were you, I'd stop talking about it. Those C.I.A. cats are liable to hear you, and you'll wind up in the Potomac yourself—with your feet in cement."

I was almost convinced that I was barking but the wrong tree.

Almost, but not quite.

There was something about his reaction that didn't sit quite right with me.

I sensed that he was rebuffing me too emphatically and too fast—as though he was *hoping* I'd believe our party-night conversation had been an hallucination.

If my hunch was right, his reluctance to talk was understandable. Four people had been garroted in New York in less than a month. For all he knew, I could be a security man high up in the conspiracy looking for fellow conspirators with loose tongues. And if I had found him to be another blabbermouth, he might become Garrote Victim Number Five.

In any case, I could see that I wasn't going to get any more information from him while he was sober. So I invited him to bring a few of his friends to my apartment later in the night for another LSP party.

He promptly turned down the offer, saying that he had a date with a non-acid-using girlfriend. The refusal left me more convinced than ever that he was part of the plot.

But how could I get him to open up to me?

I had no idea.

I only knew that I was no closer to cracking The Big

74

Freak-Out now than I had been that night in my apartment when Walrus-moustache put me on the case.

Meanwhile, the hours were ticking away and A-Day— "A" for Acid—was rapidly drawing nearer.

Angry with myself, angry with the hippies, angry with Walrus-moustache, and angry with life in general, I left The Ink Well and headed east toward St. Mark's Place. By this time it was midnight. I found a phone booth, gave Aunt Matilda a progress report and asked if she had any ideas about what I should do next. She suggested that my best bet was a good night's sleep.

It wasn't a bad idea, but I usually don't sleep very well unless I've had a little pre-slumber sexercise. So I made the rounds of a few hippie hangouts looking for someone who might be interested in playing the game. After bar-hopping for two hours without a nibble, I went back to The Ink Well to invite Lola for an after-the-gig wrestling match. Like they say, any port in a storm.

Bad Break Number Four—the port was closed. At least, to my steamboat it was. Lola had found another tourist who needed her love more than I did. I went home—and to bed—alone. It had been quite an afternoon and evening. No runs, no hits and no eros. . . .

I woke up the next morning at eleven. Since hippiedom doesn't come to life before sunset, I had the whole day to myself and I knew just what I wanted to do with it. I wanted to get as far away from the hippie scene as possible, if only to reassure myself that the rest of the world was still swinging along per usual.

I subwayed uptown to the Fifth Avenue business district. In the past, I had found this turf to be a first class girl-hunting preserve, where models, secretaries, airline hostesses, salesclerks and all sorts of other normal types strut their pretty stuff from nine to five just dying to strike up an acquaintance with the right guy.

75

Ordinarily I'd be that guy. But now, thanks to the long hair and beard I had grown to gain acceptance among the hippies. I was about as welcome as H. Rap Brown at a convention of Ku Klux Klansmen. I said "Hi" to a shapely stewardess who was waiting to catch a bus at the corner of Fifth and Fifty-Second. She scampered across the street— against the light, yet—at a speed somewhere near Mach Three. I tried the "What's-your-name?" approach next, but with a countergirl on Fifty-Sixth Street. She looked at me as if I were Typhoid Mary. Finally I smiled at a bosomy page-girl outside the N.B.C. studios at Rockefeller Center. She all but hollered for the cops.

It's a wise general who knows when to retreat. I retreated to the Forty-Second Street branch of the public library and killed the rest of the afternoon reading newspaper accounts of the James Hartley murder case.

Two days had passed now since the body of Corinne LaBelle's ex-beau had been found in Tompkins Square Park, and the police seemed no closer to a solution. Only one item in the news stories seemed significant. A short distance from the body, cops had found an envelope containing fifteen pills which under laboratory analysis had proved to be five-microgram tablets of LSD.

The papers seemed to think that this meant the killer was an acid-head who had dropped the envelope while leaving the scene of the crime. But I found it hard to believe that a hippie going out on a murder mission would carry so much acid with him.

I wondered if maybe the envelope had belonged to Hartley instead of the murderer. If that had been the case, a very interesting link would have been established between Corinne LaBelle and the hippies. And Walrus-moustache might be able to use that link to persuade the disbelieving cabinet officer who supervised the agency's operations that The Big Freak-Out was more than just a crazy acid-head's dream.

I phoned Aunt Matilda and suggested the possibility. Then I headed back to my apartment, wolfed down a steak, showered and changed. By this time it was seven o'clock, the perfect hour to make a second try at meeting with The Big Head I taxied to The Church of the Sacred Acid.

The flunky who had given me the too-busy routine the night before was at the door when I got there. I renewed my request for an audience and got another turn-down. Masking my disappointment with a smile, I wandered into the restaurant next door, ordered a cup of coffee and tried to figure out my next move.

As things now stood, I was riding a downhill curve so steep that it threatened to plummet right off the graph.

I had followed up on my only two leads, and both had led me down blind alleys.

I would've bet my virility that both The Big Head and Egbert were in on the conspiracy up to their ears, but I couldn't get close to either one of them, much less infiltrate their colleagues, because both were avoiding me as if I were a carrier of bubonic plague.

So what to do?

I thought about it.

And I thought about it some more.

Before long I had nursed down my second cup of coffee and was starting on my third Still I had no answer.

Then, suddenly, a light bulb marked "Idea!" flashed to life inside my brain.

It was a long shot, and a dangerous one.

But it just might work.

It revolved around the reversing of an old axiom to read, "If you can't join 'em, lick 'em."

Or, put more elaborately—"If the bastards won't let you play their game, make them play yours."

And I knew just how to do it.

Gulping down my third cup of coffee, I hurried back to The Church of the Sacred Acid and bought a ticket for the evening's service. It was an exact rerun of the routine I had sat through the night I went there with Lola. The Big Head knocked materialism, sang the praises of love and promised to demonstrate with Chiquita where things were really at.

I cooled my heels until the two of them went into their non-contact love bit. Then, while The Big Head was making gestures of benediction over his pretty acolyte's naked body, I slipped out of my seat and tiptoed through the darkened loft to the door leading backstage. When the lights went out, I sneaked through the door and down a narrow corridor to an oversized bathroom which evidently served as The Big Head's dressing room. I was waiting there, sitting on the toilet seat, when he and Chiquita came back to change.

They took one look at me and their faces went white. Chiquita retreated fearfully to a neutral corner. The Big Head blinked, ran his fingers through his hair, looked around, toyed with his hound's-teeth necklace and poked his hands in and out of the folds of his robe. Finally he managed to sputter, "What the hell are *you* doing here?"

I flashed a Mike Hammer grin. "Waiting for you, pal. We were supposed to have a little discussion, remember?"

He looked around again, as if trying to find a hole to crawl into. Then he pulled himself together and regarded me with the expression of a haughty personnel director getting ready to give the heave-ho to an unwelcome job applicant. "I'd like to spend some time with you, Damon," he said, "but I suddenly find myself very busy. Let me have your phone number, and I'll give you a ring when things slow down."

My grin broadened. "I can't wait that long, Worthington. I'm anxious to share my ideas with you."

He went to the mirror over the sink and began washing off his makeup. "Write me a letter about them," he smirked. "If I like what I read, you might just get an answer."

I got up from the john and positioned myself behind him. My eyes found his in the mirror. For a moment I just glowered at him and let him see that hate that was raging inside me. Then, with one quick motion, I grabbed his hair and tugged his head back until his body was arched like a bent sapling and his face was looking at me upside down. My knee found a spot midway up his spine and pressed hard against it. "Now listen, Worthington, and listen good," I hissed. "I know about The Big Freak-Out. I know when it's coming off and I know who's behind it. I know where your people are going to be stationed when they make their big move, and I know just how they're going to go about it."

He squirmed, and I dug my knee harder into his back.

"Let me go!" he gasped. "You're killing me!"

I pulled his head farther down and drove my knee farther up.

"Please!" he begged. "I don't know what you're talking about!"

I smiled and gave him a little more of the same treatment.

Tears came to his eyes and his voice was reduced to a hoarse whisper. "Please, Damon! Let me go! I'll do anything you say!"

I held on tight. "Okay, Worthington, here's what I want you to do. Go back to your bosses and tell them I want a piece of the action. One way or another I'm going to get it. If they cut me in voluntarily, we can be partners and split the pie right down the middle. If they don't, the people I'm working with are going to stage another coup a few minutes after your people stage theirs. We're a lot better equipped than you are and a lot better organized. You won't stand a chance."

79

I let go of his hair. He struggled to his feet, clutched his aching back and tried to assume an expression of outraged bewilderment. "For a sex researcher, Damon," he stammered, "you're a pretty violent type."

I let my eyes narrow into two little slits. "You ain't seen nothing yet, pal. Mess up on the little mission I just assigned you and you'll find out how violent I really can be."

He straightened his robe and leaned against the sink. "I'd like to do what you want, Damon. I really would, because frankly I'm suddenly frightened to death of you." His face showed just the right amount of fear. "But you're talking to the wrong man. I don't have any bosses to give your message to. And I don't know what the hell you're talking about with this Big Freak-Out jazz."

I brought my face close to his. "Then find out, buddy. And find out fast, because I'm coming back tomorrow night at seven. When I get here, I want that goon you've got at the door to bow and scrape and address me as 'sir' before he ushers me to your bathroom. And when I see you, you'd better have an answer for me. If it's yes, there won't be any problems. If it's no, you're going to have a million of 'em."

He started to protest, but I cut him off.

"One more thing," I said. "Don't get any ideas about sending one of your gooks with piano wire after me. I'm not alone in this thing. If one of your people kills me, you'll never live to celebrate my funeral."

His mouth was open, but no words came out. He just stood there, clutching the sink and looking scared.

I glanced at Chiquita, who was still cowering in the corner. "You were lots of fun at the party, kiddo," I told her. "Don't blow your cool and we might trip the light fantastic again when all this is over."

It was a great exit line, and I knew I'd never be able to
80

top it, so I took off before either of them had a chance to reply.

Out on the street, I made a beeline for a phone booth. When Aunt Matilda answered my call, I told her what I had done. Then I asked her to get on the line as quickly as possible with one of the agency's New York operatives. I wanted the operative to meet me at my apartment at midnight with a forty-five automatic, a shotgun and enough ammo to blow the East Village into Long Island Sound.

She promised to set things up without delay. I hung up and headed for The Ink Well.

The Decline of the West wasn't on duty, but a twenty-dollar bill persuaded the bartender to give me the name and address of every man in the group. I tried Egbert's pad first. When two minutes of pounding on the door failed to produce a reply, I headed for the next place on the list. There was no answer there either, but there was at the third place, and the guy who answered was Egbert himself.

"Come on outside," I told him. "I want to talk to you."

His dilated pupils told me that he was flying higher than a Boeing 707. "Sorry, baby, I'm busy," he mumbled. "Catch me some other time."

I caught him all right—by the throat. His eyes bulged and the veins in his forehead threatened to burst as I bore down on his adam's apple and swung him around into the hallway. "I don't like rude creeps, creep," I said. "And you're a rude creep."

I squeezed harder and his face turned dark red. Then his mouth popped open, and an unintelligible little squeal came out. I loosened my grip enough to let him try again. "I'm sorry," he gasped. "Honest, I'm sorry."

I let him go. He dropped to the floor, clutching his throat. I buried my heel in his chest to keep him there. "Egbert," I said, "you can't hold your acid, and a man who can't hold his acid is a danger to the movement."

His eyes found mine, and suddenly he seemed very sober. "Wh-what do you mean?" he asked.

"You know damned well what I mean. The other night at the party you told me all about The Big Freak-Out. Me, a complete stranger. How'd you know I wasn't with the F.B.I.?"

"You were w-with L-lola," he stuttered. "I f-figured you were all r-r-right."

"But you didn't figure I was all right last night when I saw you at The Ink Well."

"I-I was s-s-scared. I d-didn't like the way you c-c-came on."

I took my foot off him and let him get to his feet. He brushed off, leaned against the bannister and looked at me as though he were afraid I was going to breathe fire on him.

"Egbert," I said, "you're damned lucky you opened your mouth to me and not to somebody else. Four other creeps in this town opened their mouths to the wrong people, and now all four of them are dead. You'd be dead too if you didn't cover up so well last night, but now that I've seen that you can think on your feet, I'm not going to kill you."

"Thanks," he managed.

I pretended I didn't hear him. "Besides," I went on, "I've got other plans for you. You're too stoned tonight to talk sensibly, so I'll wait till tomorrow to tell you what I have in mind. Meanwhile, I'm telling you now that I want you to stay straight until the time our thing swings into action. And I mean completely straight. No acid, no coke, no hash. Not even pot. Get it?"

He nodded.

I gestured toward the door. "You can go back inside now. But I'll stop by your pad tomorrow to talk more. Understand?"

He got off a weak "Yeah."

I tossed him a look that'd wilt an onion, then scampered down the stairs.

My watch said five after eleven. I phoned Aunt Matilda to find out if my order for the guns and the ammo had been put through. She reported that it had. I thanked her and ducked into a nearby bar for a quick beer. Then I took a slow walk across town to my apartment, timing it so that I'd get there at exactly twelve.

My timing was perfect. So was the timing of the little guy who came staggering down the street from the opposite direction.

He was wearing workman's white coveralls and a cap, the bill of which all but buried his face. The reason he was staggering was the enormous box he had hoisted over one of his shoulders. It was all of four feet long, three feet wide and two feet deep.

"Wheah else but in dis stoopid boig wouldja fine a joik dat wants a TV set so bad he's willing ta cough up an extra hunnert bucks fer immediate delivery?" he asked me in a loud, obviously phony Brooklyn accent. "And wheah else wouldja fine a bum like my boss dat's so hungry fer a buck dat he wakes me outta my goilfriend's bed alla way ova in Greenpernt just ta deliva it? You wooden happen ta know wheah a guy named Rod Damon lives, wouldja buddy?"

I peered beneath the peak of his cap. He scowled at me, and his small white teeth glinted ferociously beneath his walrus-like moustache. "Don't just stand there, you idiot!" he hissed. "Open the door! This box is heavy."

We carried the box up the stairs together. Inside my apartment, he pried off the top. Then, like a magician pulling rabbits out of a hat, he produced two forty-five automatics, a twelve-gauge shotgun, a twenty-gauge shotgun, a thirty-caliber submachine gun and nine boxes of ammunition.

"I've got to give you credit," I told him. "You really believe that what's worth doing is worth doing well."

He dismissed the compliment with a shrug. "If I interpreted Aunt Matilda's message correctly, you're going

83

to need all this and more. What are you trying to do? Get yourself killed?"

I smiled. "A forty-five is pretty good protection against a man with a strand of piano wire, isn't it?"

He scowled. "Not if he gets the wire around your neck before you get a chance to pull the forty-five."

I gulped. "Maybe trying to force their hand wasn't such a good idea after all."

He regarded me with a look of grudging admiration. "Well, Damon, it wasn't the textbook solution to the problem, but frankly it was a brilliant idea. Dangerous, perhaps; but brilliant. Also, judging from developments of the past week, quite necessary. You see, we now believe that a target date has been set for The Big Freak-Out, and it's right around the proverbial corner."

"Tell me more."

"As you know, you're not the only operative our agency has on this case. Others have been keeping a close watch on suspicious hippies in San Francisco, Chicago and Miami as well as New York. Two days ago, a contingent of hippies from all four of these cities arrived in Washington. Yesterday another contingent arrived. Today, still another. All told, there are now nearly sixty-five hippies in the capital whom we suspect of involvement in the plot. Presumably this is the advance force, whose function is to set things up for the main body of troops, who'll arrive in a day or two and make their move a day or two after that."

I whistled under my breath. "You think it's that close?"

"Yes, and here's why. We've just learned from a source high up in the State Department that an ultra-top-secret and ultra-high-level diplomatic conference has been set between representatives of the United States and representatives of Communist China. The conference is scheduled to begin on the twenty-third, just nine days from today. It's my theory that The Big Freak-out has been timed to break anywhere from one to four days after the conference."

"I don't get it. If the Chinese want to meet us at the conference table, why would they back a plot to overthrow our government? Obviously we won't be in a position to discuss anything if Washington is in total chaos."

"That's the whole point. The people who are backing the plot actually want to sabotage the conference."

"Then why agree to confer in the first place?"

He smiled sardonically. "The answer to that lies in the crazy-quilt maze of China's internal politics. But, before I get started on that, I want a drink."

I poured a healthy one for each of us. He downed half of his in a single swallow, smacked his lips and plunged into the promised dissertation.

"As you probably realize, Red China today harbors two political factions, the extremists and the so-called moderates. To the Western eye, they appear similar to the point of being merely the same product in two different packages. Actually, however, they're quite dissimilar. Both naturally are opposed to capitalism and seek to convert the world to communism. But the moderates argue that China is not now strong enough to risk an out-and-out confrontation with the capitalist powers, whereas the extremists maintain that she is strong enough. So far, the moderates have prevailed. But the extremists are rapidly gaining popular support, and some knowledgeable observers feel that the balance of power will soon swing their way."

"Where does Mao fit into the picture?"

"He's on the fence. Despite the image of domestic omnipotence which he has managed to convey, he's presently struggling very hard to keep his hold on things. That's why he didn't crack down when the Red Guards went on a rampage a few months ago, and it's why he didn't intervene when Lin Po needed his help. According to my sources in the State Department, he'll go whichever way the wind blows."

85

"Very interesting."

"Yes, and also very dangerous. At least, it is for us."

"I don't follow you."

"Well, if he had a tighter hold on things, we'd know pretty much what to expect from him. As it is, we're completely in the dark."

"Point taken. But how does all this tie in with the conference you were talking about?"

"The conference was set up by the moderates, who more or less control China's Department of State. Presumably they're going to spell out their problems for us and ask us to make a gesture of peace—maybe a slowdown in Vietnam—so that they can regain some of the ground they've recently lost to the extremists. It would benefit us to do so, of course, because we're as eager to avoid a confrontation at this time as they are."

"And The Big Freak-Out?"

"That's the extremists' baby. They control the Army and the Espionage Corps. We think they had the plan in the works for some time before the conference was set up and are now adjusting their schedule to achieve maximum political effect at home as well as abroad."

"So, when all is said and done, the extremists and the moderates are playing a game of political Chinese checkers, and the United States is the pawn."

"Precisely, and also the prize. That's why your little power play with The Big Head may prove to be a stroke of sheer genius. When he tells his bosses that you've got a conspiracy going that plans to steal *his* conspiracy's thunder, they won't know which way to turn. If they still want to stage their coup before the conference, they'll have to come out in the open and find out just what you've got going for you. If they don't come out into the open, they'll have to delay the coup. One way or the other, we're ahead of the game. Your ploy has purchased us an invaluable tactical advantage."

"But," I pointed out, remembering his advice about the possibility of a man's getting some piano wire around my neck before I could pull my forty-five, "the purchase price may have been my life."

"Unfortunately, yes." His tone became solemn. "And if that's the case, Damon, we'll all miss you very much."

"How consoling."

He drained his drink and handed me the empty glass. "But," he said, his face suddenly brightening, "let's look at the positive side of the picture. We're no longer in the dark. The fat is in the fire. We can expect action at any moment, and"—he patted the barrel of the submachinegun—"we're ready for it."

"I wish," I murmured candidly, "I could share your enthusiasm."

He got up from his chair, inspected his coveralls and tugged the bill of his cap over his eyes. "You will. Just wait till the bullets start flying." He started toward the door. "And now, much as I enjoy your company, I must be off. Is there anything I can do for you while I'm in Washington?"

"Yeah. Assign another agent to the case."

"Heh-heh. Very funny, Damon. *Very* funny. You have a natural talent for comedy. Did anyone ever tell you that?" His hand found the doorknob. "Ta-ta, now. And happy hunting."

"Wait," I said. Suddenly I remembered my man Egbert, of the Decline of the West. As of the moment, he was convinced that I was a fellow conspirator. But he'd be infinitely more useful if he could be persuaded to work along with me knowing exactly who I was and whom I represented. With Walrus-moustache's help, I might be able to persuade him.

Walrus-moustache turned from the door. "Did I hear you say 'wait'?" he asked.

"Yeah. There's nothing you can do for me in Washing-

87

ton, but you just might be able to do something in New York."

"For example?"

"Do you have any connections among Federal narcotics men?"

"A few."

I wrote Egbert's name and address on a slip of paper. "I want this guy picked up on a dope charge—any dope charge—and I want him held incommunicado until I come to rescue him. Do you think you can arrange it?"

"The American Civil Liberties Union won't like it, but I'll see what I can do." He tucked the slip of paper into the pocket of his coveralls. "Phone Aunt Matilda tomorrow at noon. She'll tell you what jail they're holding him at and what officer to contact to spring him." He opened the door. "Anything else I can do for you?"

"Not for the present."

He grinned. "Then, cheerio. And keep smiling. I think we can safely predict that the spit will hit the fan soon."

"Yeah," I replied grimly, still thinking of piano wire. "It's a pretty safe prediction."

CHAPTER 6

It was.

Walrus-moustache had hardly left the apartment when my doorbell rang. I peered through the peephole and found myself looking into the flashing eyes of Chiquita. With her was another sexy latin—a few inches shorter, darker, probably half Negro, and every bit as tittilating.

I grabbed a forty-five in one hand and opened the door with the other. Chiquita looked at the gun without flinching, then rolled her sexy eyes at me. "Like, wow," she said, her slight Spanish accent giving the hippie jargon a cute sound, "talk about a gracious host."

I let the barrel of the forty-five graze menacingly across the upthrust tips of her unholstered thirty-eights. "Security, sweetie," I explained. "If you're not packing any piano wire, you don't have anything to fear."

"The only piano wire I have is in my piano, Damon. Now are you going to let us in, or do you want to stand in the doorway all night pointing that thing at us?"

I took a step backward and motioned with the gun toward the couch. "Make yourselves comfortable, but don't make any sudden moves. When I shoot, I aim for the heart. I'd hate to mess up all that luscious upholstery."

Chiquita and her companion sat down. I locked the door, then flopped into a chair opposite them. The forty-five scanned across their breasts like a radar screen scanning the sky.

89

"Okay," I said, "what's the message from The Big Head?"

Chiquita gave me a hurt look. "Does there have to be a message? Couldn't I have come over here just because I wanted to see you?"

"You could have. But did you?"

"Yes."

"Why?"

"I liked what we did together that night at the party. I want to do it again."

"And your friend here?"

"She wants to do it too."

"A likely story," I clichéd.

Chiquita sighed and her magnificent mammaries strained against the gauze-thin fabric of her blouse. "What's with you, Damon? You're supposed to be a lover, not a fighter. Why don't you put that stupid gun away and give us what we came for?"

I smiled. "Because I'm still not sure what you came for."

"Sex. That's all. Now will you please put that gun away? It's making me very nervous."

"How do I know that when I do you won't pull some piano wire out from under that miniskirt and give me a G-string necktie?"

She sighed again, harder this time, and her succulent breasts threatened to burst right through her blouse. "Oh, for heaven's sake, Damon, the only thing under my miniskirt is. . . ." She let the sentence trail off. Her eyes found mine. She tried a new tack. "Look, Damon. You're supposed to be a sex expert. Can't you tell a passionate girl when you see one? If you're so worried about piano wire, Carla and I'll take off all our clothes. Would that convince you?"

"It wouldn't be a bad idea," I admitted.

Chiquita barked a few words in Spanish and both girls promptly began to undress. I sat back and watched.

90

It was quite a sight.

The two Latin lovelies were as stacked as a traveling card sharp's blackjack deck, and they moved with the precision of a pair of Rockettes.

First, two sets of hands made short work of unbuttoning two blouses. The buttons fell away, revealing the bulging insides of two pairs of splendiferous spheres.

Then, two right arms shot into the air and two left hands urged two right sleeves over them. Neither girl was wearing a bra, with the result that two breasts lay completely exposed, bright orange nipples jutting out like a pair of bullets.

Next, the newly unsleeved right arms proceeded to unsleeve the left arms. The blouses dropped to the floor, and my beauties stood completely bare from the waist up. The new girl's tan globes were like two ripe fruits just begging to be squeezed, pinched and touched.

Now it was time for the miniskirts. Two right hands tugged at two buckles. The buckles unbuckled, the zippers beneath them were unzipped. Like two firemen sliding down two poles, the two minis slid down the luxurious pillars that were the girls' legs and landed in a heap at their ankles.

Chiquita had been telling the truth. The only thing under her mini was *her*—and she was delectable. Her companion was no slouch either. The smooth lines of both girls' bellies, hips and thighs were an engraved invitation for further exploration.

"Doesn't anybody wear underwear anymore?" I managed.

The only reply was a smile from Chiquita. Then, resuming the Rockette bit, the cuddlesome cuties executed a pair of back-kicks that sent the minis flying onto the couch. I surveyed the scene, grinned my approval and lowered my forty-five.

"Well," said Chiquita, "are you going to show Carla and

me to your bedroom? Or would you rather entertain us here?"

I was still far from convinced that the only purpose of their visit was sex. But they certainly seemed harmless enough standing there in their birthday suits, and sex was as good a way as any to pass the time while I tried to figure out what they really had come for. "In the bedroom," I said, ushering them inside. Then I latched the door, put the forty-five on a shelf that would be out of their reach if they decided to make a grab for it and prepared to give them what they said they wanted.

Chiquita and Carla sat side by side on the edge of the bed.

I approached them and Chiquita's hand found my belt buckle. Carla went to work on my zipper. Her fingers brushed against the stiffness beneath it, and she turned to Chiquita with an expression of pleasant surprise.

"*Ya?*" she asked. "*Carramba!*"

"*Siempre,*" replied Chiquita. "*Es bueno, verdad?*" To me she explained, "Carla's surprised that you're ready. I told her you always are."

I hadn't needed the translation, but I saw no point in letting them know about my fluency in their language. "Tell her it's a biological quirk," I said. "Priapism."

She translated, and Carla's curiosity was satisfied. Both girls then returned to the matter at hand.

Chiquita helped me out of one trouser leg while Carla helped me out of the other. My shoes impeded their progress, so they took them off. Then they went to work on my socks, shorts and shirt. In seconds I was as naked as they were.

Carla positioned herself horizontally across the head of the bed, and Chiquita maneuvered me into place at a diagonal to her. I lay on my back, with Carla's breasts serving as my pillow. My legs dangled over the side of the bed, and my feet touched the floor. Chiquita knelt between them.

Carla's breasts were a sea of warm, tender, sweet-smelling flesh. She squeezed her arms alongside them, and they wrapped themselves lovingly around my face. Their hot red tip: were barely an inch from my lips. Then, in a flash, they were in my mouth.

I nibblec at them hungrily. My tongue traced circles around the nipples, and my teeth raked across the soft, firm mounds fron which they projected. Soft purrs of contentment coming from Carla's throat assured me that my efforts weren't going unnoticed. The insistent pressure of her gently undulating womanhood against my shoulder reinforced the impression.

But Carla didn't have a monopoly on my attention. As Chiquita knelt between my legs, her tongue drew warm, wet patterns across my belly. At the same time, her small and skillful fingers fluttered up and down my manhood. They squeezed and stroked, kneaded and pressed, teased and caressed.

Soon her mouth joined her fingers. The sensation was exquisite. Tantalizing flames of pleasure burned through my loins. A volcano of excitement welled up inside me.

I gnawed all the more hungrily on Carla's breasts. In reply, she brought her mouth to the nape of my neck and began chewing on my ear. My hand stroked the insides of her thighs, which spread eagerly. My thumb found her womanhood and slowly inched inside. It was met with an overflowing of passion.

"Do you like it?" I heard Chiquita ask.

The sweet pain of Carla's bite choked off my words. I squirmed, and my hips went into a gentle dance about Chiquita's mouth. My passion grew and grew.

Chiquita realized that I was rapidly approaching the point of no return. Her mouth undulated. My body arched

93

high, then came down only to rise even higher. The tide of burning passion welled up within me.

Carla didn't want to get left out of things. Slipping out from beneath me, she dug her knees into the mattress on one side of my head and her fists into the mattress on the other. Her breasts swayed tantalizingly over my face.

I licked at them, and her body swayed slightly forward. Then I tongued her tummy, and she swayed a little more. I knew what she wanted, and I didn't mind letting her have it. My tongue found its way across the soft, smooth moss shielding her womanhood. Then her entire body shook with delight as my lips caressed her.

An inferno of hot breath and writhing bodies surrounded me. Chiquita's lips were moving faster and faster. She moved from side to side, up and down, back and forth. At the same time, my tongue probed Carla.

The sensations were too exquisite to last, and they didn't. Heaving mightily, I let loose a flow of love, the spasms of which shook the bodies of both my Latin lovelies.

When it was over, the three of us lay together, the girls' bodies bracketing mine like parentheses. Carla gently tongued my neck, while Chiquita's teeth toyed with my ear. Both girls' hands stroked my abdomen and explored the hair on my chest.

Finally Chiquita said, "You're beautiful, Damon. Too beautiful for words."

"You're not bad yourself," I conceded. "And neither is your girlfriend." Then, remembering the circumstances under which the three of us were gathered, I added, "But I still can't believe that sex is the only purpose of your visit."

Chiquita sounded disappointed. "Why not?"

"It seems to me that you'd get all the loving you wanted from the crowd at The Church of the Sacred Acid, especially from the ever-lovin' Big Head."

"Ha!" she spat. "And you're supposed to be a sex

expert?! For your information, The Big Head hasn't touched me once in the whole six months I've been his mistress!"

My ears perked up.

"He talks about love," she went on. "He talks about it all the time. But all he does is talk." She mimicked his voice. " 'Love so sure, so confident, so absolutely certain of itself that it needs no physical expression!' " Her own voice returned. "My father's moustache! The Big Head couldn't express his love physically if his life depended on it!"

"You mean he's impotent?"

"I don't know what he is. I only know what he does, which is nothing. At least, not to me."

"Maybe he has other girlfriends?"

"I don't think so. I'd know about it if he did."

"How about boyfriends?" I asked.

"No. None of them either. There was a guy who used to hang around The Church sometimes, a Black Muslim named Swami Swahili. I thought for a while that The Big Head might've been sweet on him, but he took off more than a month ago and I haven't seen him since. If The Big Head misses him, he doesn't let on."

My hand found her breast and began stroking it. In reply, she snuggled against me. As if on cue, Carla joined in on the action, wrapping her legs around one of mine and stroking my manhood with her fingers.

For the present, however, I was more interested in the conversation than the sex-play. "So you're The Big Head's mistress," I mused. "And he doesn't make love to you. Very interesting."

"Also very sad, if one happens to be a hot-blooded young lady—which I am."

My eyebrows arched quizzically. "Then why don't you leave him?"

"Money, Damon. It's the only thing that keeps us together." She sighed. "When my family came to this

95

country a year ago from Puerto Rico, we expected all sorts of wonderful opportunities. We were soon disillusioned. My father couldn't find work and we had to go on relief. All seven of us—my father, my mother, my baby brother, my three sisters and I—lived in a four-room apartment that was crawling with rats. We didn't even have our own toilet. We had to share the one in the hallway with three other families."

I clucked sympathetically.

She raised herself on one elbow. Her eyes burned imploringly into mine. "Then," she said, "my father died. The funeral expenses put our family horribly in debt. My mother didn't speak English and couldn't get a job. My baby brother was only four years old. I was the head of the family, and I didn't know where to turn. That's when I met The Big Head. He liked me and he asked me to come and live with him. I knew that anything would be better than the apartment I was living in with my family, so I said yes. He and I lived together, and he gives me lots of money. I was frugal with it from the first, and soon I had saved enough to rent my family a very nice apartment. They live there now. and they enjoy all the conveniences they have always desired They even have a TV set. Meanwhile, I continue to live with The Big Head. He gives me a hundred dollars a week spending money. I keep ten for myself and give the rest to my mother. It may not be a very honorable way for a girl to support her family, but it's the way I've chosen and I'm not ashamed of it."

I eyed her skeptically. "A very touching story, Chiquita. Plenty of drama, plenty of pathos. Even a smash, no-regrets ending " My tones were acid. "But I'm not buying it. You're as phony as a fifty-cent diamond ring."

Her mouth popped open in disbelief of my disbelief. "What do you mean?"

"The story doesn't wash, honey. There're too many holes in it. For one thing, you say you came to the United

96

States only a year ago. But you speak better English than some people who've lived here all their lives."

"I studied English in school at San Juan."

"For another, a hundred dollars a week is an awful lot of money for a man to give to a girl he doesn't make love to. What's The Big Head's angle in keeping you as his mistress?"

"I'm useful to him at The Church of the Sacred Acid. You saw me there the other night. He needs me for his act."

"Still, if money's all you're after, I'm sure you could find a sugar daddy who has a lot more of it than The Big Head."

"You think so, huh? Well, you've got another think coming. Remember, this is New York and I'm a Puerto Rican. We have never been considered very desirable by men who like to think of themselves as 'pure' Americans." She lowered her voice. "Besides, even though The Big Head doesn't satisfy me sexually, I like him. He's a very warm and gentle man, and he's a man of principle. He's sacrificed everything he's ever had just so he could go out among the people and preach his doctrines of love."

"Come on, now. No chick that manipulates a guy for a hundred clams a week is going to tell me that she falls for the line he hands out at The Church of the Sacred Acid."

"I believe heart and soul in what he says, Damon. And I believe in *him*. He may not be a great lover, but he's a great leader. The world will soon recognize that. Just wait and see."

I shrugged. I still wasn't buying her story. But I wasn't in the mood for debate. "Okay, he's a great leader. And you think very highly of him. I have just one more question. Knowing what you know about my relationship with him, what're you doing here in my bedroom? Doesn't our little tete-a-tete strike you as slightly disloyal?"

She smiled prettily. "Not at all. You see, I told him I was

97

coming to see you. He approved."

"I don't get it. A few hours ago I gave him a pretty rough time. Tomorrow night, he's going to get an even rougher time unless he's prepared to deliver what my buddies and I want from him. Now you're telling me that you asked his permission to go to bed with me and he said yes?"

"That's right. You see, we have an arrangement. Since he can't satisfy me sexually, he permits me to make love to whoever I choose."

"Even if the man you choose happens to be his sworn enemy?"

"The Big Head has no enemies, Damon. He loves everyone—even those who abuse him."

I decided to abandon the conversation. I still wasn't buying her story, but I was tired of riding a merry-go-round of cop-outs and contradictions. If she had come to my apartment for more than sexual satisfaction, she'd let me know about it in her own good time. Meanwhile, if sex was all she was after, I'd give her her fill of it.

I lay silently on the bed. She lowered herself back into place against me. Her fingers began stroking my thigh. Her lips found my neck and began nibbling on it. Carla, who had remained at my side without a whimper through the entire discussion, automatically picked up where she had left off when the talking began.

A minute passed. Then a minute more. Then Chiquita got a bright idea. She told Carla about it in Spanish.

I listened closely and I understood every word, but when all the words were strung together they didn't make sense. All I could get out of the exchange was that Chiquita and Carla were going to entertain me with what they called a *pasa doble*. Literally, that translates as "double step" or "two step." It's the name of a popular Latin-American dance.

But whatever gave them the idea that I wanted to dance? Or to watch them dance? And if they weren't talking about

98

dancing, what were they talking about?

I soon found out.

Their conversation was over, the two beauties urged my legs over the side of the bed and knelt on the floor at my feet. Then Chiquita brought her lips to one ankle and Carla brought hers to the other. They began kissing their way upward.

Their tongues made hot, wet circles alongside the insides of my calves and thighs. Before long they had reached the point beyond which it was impossible to go. Chiquita's right hand and Carla's left closed simultaneously around my quivering pillar. Their fingers interlocked, and they squeezed hard. Meanwhile, their tongues went to work on the area beneath.

So that's what they meant by *pasa doble!*

It wasn't a new method.

If I remembered correctly, the Roman historian, Suetonius, had mentioned in *Lives of the Twelve Caesars* that Emperor Tiberius used to conscript peasant children to perform it on him.

Also, I'd had it performed on me once during the course of a sexual study I was conducting at a brothel in Havana, where my partners had referred to it by a Spanish term considerably less delicate than *pasa doble.*

But that had been way back in 1958, and my memory of the occasion was dim. Now Chiquita and Carla were giving me a second chance to see what it was all about. I propped myself up on my elbows to get a better look.

What I saw made me even more excited than what I felt. The two coppertone cuties had their pretty faces together. While tonguing me, they also were kissing each other. Their eyes were squeezed shut. The soft, smooth skin of their cheeks pressed tenderly against my loins. Their coal-black hair fell behind them, covering the deed like a curtain.

My hips automatically began moving slowly back and

99

forth. In reply, the girls released their grip on my manhood. Then their mouths moved into place where their fingers had been. Still kissing each other as much as they were kissing me, they raced wildly over the swollen organ's entire surface.

Electric tongues of sensation tore through me. My body was taut, high-tension wire. I heard myself moan, and the boiling lava of my passion bubbled up inside me.

The girls knew what was happening. They let go of me instantly. Carla, leaping to her feet impaled herself on me. Chiquita crawled between my legs and goaded me on with her tongue.

I tried to keep a tight rein on myself. Carla had shown me a good time and I wanted to reciprocate. Biting my lip to take my mind off the sensations in my groin, I assaulted her with long, deep, body-jarring strokes. She jounced around on top of me, her fingernails digging hungrily into my thighs, her enormous breasts jiggling wildly before her.

I knew I couldn't hold on much longer. Every thrust of her hips set off a new spark inside me. The boiling lava bubbled higher. The earthshaking tremors of eruption were beginning.

Carla jounced all the harder. Her head was tossed back. Her body was twisted into a tense spiral. Biting more deeply into my lip, I matched her stroke for stroke.

Beneath me, Chiquita was still doing her bit. Her hot, wet tongue darted across whatever part of my fast-moving chassis she could get it on. Her fingers probed my buttocks. Her teeth dug into the soft flesh inside my thighs.

I was at the edge of the ledge, but fortunately, so was Carla. For a moment we hovered there together. Then, with breasts shaking wildly and legs scissoring frantically, she went off.

That was all I needed. Like a thunderhead cracking across the sky, my body exploded into a spasm of overwhelming sensation.

Finally it was over. I stretched out on the bed, exhausted. Carla slid into place alongside me. Chiquita found a spot on the other side. For all of five minutes, we lay there without saying a word. Then Chiquita got up.

"Well, Damon," she smiled, "it really was a pleasure. Now, with your permission, my sister and I'll be on our way."

I gulped. "Carla is your sister? She's darker."

"Yes. Do you find that so unusual? Who knows who her papa was?"

I swallowed my astonishment. "Not really. The way things've been going lately, I don't find *anything* unusual. But I'm rather surprised you're leaving so soon. I thought you might like to stay and talk awhile."

"No. I promised The Big Head I'd get home early. Besides, what's there to talk about?"

My voice was dripping with sarcasm. "Well, there's the weather. And the war in Vietnam. And civil rights. And the peace movement. And if we get tired of these topics, there's always The Big Freak-Out."

"Sorry, Damon. I'm not much of a talker. But if you want to see me again, come over to The Big Head's apartment tomorrow afternoon and I'll play the piano for you." She reached for the doorlatch.

I blocked her. "Now look, Chiquita. Your boyfriend is in serious trouble. If——"

She touched a finger to my lips. "Sorry, Damon," she silenced me. "I don't meddle in The Big Head's business affairs—just like he doesn't meddle in my sexual ones. Now will you let us out, or do you plan on keeping us prisoner tonight?"

I shrugged. Unbelievable as it seemed, sex *had* been the only purpose of her visit—or, if there was another one, she had accomplished it without my knowing about it.

I opened the door and ushered the swinging sisters into the living room. Holding my forty-five for good luck, I

101

watched them dress. Then I showed them out.

"Thanks, Damon," said Chiquita at the threshold. "I enjoyed it immensely, and so did my sister. Are you going to visit me tomorrow?"

"You were serious about that?"

"Of course. I'd like very much to see you, and to play the piano for you. We could make love also, if you'd like."

"And what'll The Big Head do while we're making it? Watch?"

She chuckled softly. "He won't be there. He plans to be out all afternoon on business." She snapped open her purse, pulled out a notebook and scribbled down an address. "This is where you'll find me. Do come, won't you?"

"I'll think about it."

She flashed a warm smile, then mumbled something in Spanish to Carla. Giggling like two schoolgirls, they scampered through the hall and down the stairs. I holstered my forty-five, double-locked the door and poured myself a stiff Scotch and soda. Then I flopped down on the couch and tried to make some sense out of what had happened.

Someplace out there in The City That Never Sleeps, the local branch of The Hippies' Ad Hoc Committee for The Big Freak-Out was putting the finishing touches on a plot to overthrow the United States government. The man whom Walrus-moustache had pegged as their leader, The Big Head, was among them. Unless he had nerves of cast iron, he was worried sick that I was going to upset his little applecart.

Yet, his mistress had just spent a couple hours in bed with me—with his permission, so she said—and claimed that her only motive was sexual satisfaction.

She hadn't tried to work out a deal on his behalf.

She hadn't pumped me for information.

When I had mentioned The Big Freak-Out, she had flatly refused to discuss it.

102

And to top it all off she had invited me to The Big Head's apartment the next afternoon to listen to her play the piano.

I couldn't believe that she had visited me only because she was passionate. But I couldn't imagine what else might have impelled her to come calling.

Had she just wanted to case my apartment for The Big Head? Maybe. But I was betting against it. If The Big Head wanted to know anything about my apartment, he could find out easily enough by asking Lola.

Then, maybe the whole thing was just a way of setting me up for a meeting at The Big Head's apartment the next afternoon. But if that was what Chiquita had in mind, she went about it in the worst possible way. She could've phoned and said she wanted to meet me there. I probably would've come running.

By telling me *after* we had made love, she had destroyed the element of suspense. I really had no reason to go— unless I wanted to hear her play the piano.

Which I didn't.

And now that I thought about it, why had she stressed the piano bit so much? All told, she had mentioned it on three different occasions. Did she think I was some kind of music nut? Or was she trying to tell me something else?

Piano.

Piano wire.

An interesting avenue of speculation. But was there really a connection?

If so, what was it?

If Chiquita was trying to warn me that I *shouldn't* visit The Big Head's apartment, why did she invite me in the first place?

Because The Big Head had told her to, and because he had sent Carla along to make sure she did?

But Carla didn't speak English.

Or did she?

103

If she didn't, Chiquita wouldn't have had to invite me.

If she did, the piano bit would have been as obvious to her as it was to me.

Carla.

Where did she fit into the picture?

Was she really Chiquita's sister?

They looked enough alike that she might have been.

But wasn't the *pasa doble* a rather odd enterprise for two sisters to pursue?

They weren't only kissing me when they went through their paces. They were kissing each other.

Incest?

Well, if you incest—uh, insist.

And homosexual incest to boot.

Homosexual.

Was Chiquita homosexual?

Was The Big Head homosexual?

The more I thought about it, the more confusing it became.

But then, everything connected with The Big Freak-Out was confusing.

When I went to the party with Lola, The Big Head had come on to me like a vacuum cleaner salesman coming on to a housewife.

A day later he wouldn't touch me with a ten-foot stick of marijuana.

Egbert had cornered me in the kitchen and given me the lowdown on the whole plot.

A day later he was giving me a fourteen-karat brushoff.

Egbert's brushoff I could understand. He had spilled the beans about The Big Freak-Out while he was on LSP. Then, remembering the four hippies who had been garroted, he had tried to cover his tracks.

But why had The Big Head gone cold on me?

He hadn't told me anything at the party.

Or had he told me something while I was too high on LSP to realize it?

Or had I said or done something during my LSP high— something I no longer remembered—which made him decide I shouldn't be taken into his confidence?

I could only guess.

And my guesses were leading me nowhere.

Back to the party.

Unless I had been hallucinating, I had seen Corinne LaBelle.

What was she doing there?

Was she a prisoner of the Red Chinese who were backing the plot?

Unlikely. Since when do prisoners get invited to parties?

But, if she wasn't a prisoner, what was she doing there?

Back to the Red Chinese.

Where did they fit into the picture?

Walrus-moustache seemed to think that they were backing the plot.

But what was their line of communication to the hippies?

If there was one race of people I very definitely did not see in my travels through hippiedom, it was the oriental race.

True, as Walrus-moustache had suggested, they might have been using American or European contact men.

But who were these contact men?

And *where* were they?

For the moment, I couldn't even guess. I wasn't close enough to the scene to tell the players apart without a scorecard, let alone tell the coaches from the players!

So much for the Red Chinese.

What about James Hartley?

He was a dead-end street if ever I'd come across one.

And speaking of dead-end streets, what about that

sweetly perfumed, miniskirted cutie I'd played sex games with the night Lola and I listened to The Big Head's sermon?

I was sure when I spotted her in the aisle after the sermon that I had seen her face somewhere before.

But where?

And why hadn't I seen her since?

The whole thing was more confusing than a Chinese box puzzle.

And each new development made it more confusing still.

For a moment I wondered if it was possible that there was no conspiracy after all—that The Big Freak-Out was some sort of grotesque non-phenomenon that came into being as a result of a few hallucinations by widely scattered acid-heads and an overzealous interpretation by Walrus-moustache and his crew.

That, evidently, was exactly the impression of the high Cabinet officer who supervised the agency's operations.

And if he thought so, knowing what he knows, why shouldn't I think so, knowing what I know?

Then I remembered: I knew something he didn't know.

Egbert had so much as confessed to being part of the plot. Not only at the party where I had passed out the LSP, but also a few hours ago when I took him down off an acid high, told him I was a fellow conspirator and threatened to garrote him if he didn't keep his nose clean.

Yes, Egbert had confessed, when he had nothing to gain by doing so and a great deal to lose. And that, from where I sat, was evidence enough that the conspiracy was very real.

Now what to do about it?

I glanced at my watch.

Three fifteen.

Not much to do about it at this hour, but dawn would bring another day, and who could tell what goodies the day might have in store?

A meeting with The Big Head at seven in the evening.

106

A meeting during the afternoon with his mistress, if I chose to take her up on her invitation.

And a meeting earlier still with Egbert, if Walrus-moustache hadn't let me down.

I finished my drink, deposited the empty glass in the kitchen, and went to bed.

CHAPTER 7

Walrus-moustache hadn't let me down. When I checked in with Aunt Matilda at noon, she informed me that Egbert was being held at the Federal Detention Unit on Foley Square. The charge was "unlawful possession of narcotics." The G-Man who would serve as my contact was one Detective Marbello.

I hailed a cab to the detention unit. Marbello did a doubletake when he caught sight of my beard and long hair, but he became very friendly after I told him who I was. We walked back to the cell area together. Leading me to the dingy cubicle which was Egbert's home away from home, he locked the door and ushered me inside. "I'll be right down the corridor if you want me," he said.

I gave Egbert my best Ipana smile. He didn't smile back. His face was still frozen in the expression of astonishment which it had assumed when he first spotted me walking down the corridor with Marbello.

"Hi, Eg," I said amiably. "What's new in the music business?"

He managed to get his mouth and eyes back into working order. "Jeez, Damon," he said softly. "What're you doing here?"

I played the moment for all it was worth. "I came to talk to you, Eg. You feel up to a little chat?"

His eyes darted from my face to my fingers and back to my face. Evidently he was looking for piano wire. "Don't

108

try anything funny, Damon," he warned feebly. "I'll call a cop."

"It won't do you any good, Egbert. They're on my side."

"Who're you trying to kid? You might have the Big Head and some of the hippies in your pocket, but you don't have the G-Men there."

"You miss the point. I *am* a G-Man, baby. That's the name of the game."

His eyes widened. A nervous tic tugged at the corner of his mouth. For a moment he said nothing. Then, under his breath, he murmured, "You gotta be kiddin'."

I flashed my Ipana smile again. "You saw the detective bring me back here. They don't do that, you know, if a guy just walks in off the street and asks to see somebody."

He lowered his head, and his shoulders slumped forward in a gesture of defeat. "I know," he admitted softly. "I been busted before—in Brooklyn. My own mother couldn't get in to see me." His head slowly came up until his eyes were even with mine. "So you're a G-Man," he shrugged. "What can I do for you?"

I paced the cell as I imagined Lee Marvin might if he were playing a G-Man in a movie. "You can do a lot for me, Egbert. And I can do a lot for you. First let's talk about what I can do for you."

He watched, apparently very impressed with my routine, and waited for me to continue.

"You're in trouble, Egbert," I told him. "There's a narcotics charge against you, and if I give the right people the word, there'll be a lot of other charges against you. The main one to think about is 'conspiracy to overthrow the United States government.' It carries a prison term of twenty to forty years, and federal judges aren't as lenient as the ones at state and local levels. Dig the message?"

"I dig," he replied wearily.

"And that's only the start of your troubles. You know what happened to the four other hippies who talked." I pantomimed a piano-wire garroting. "All I've got to do is leak word to the wrong people that you're here in jail singing your brains out. When you walk out the door, your life won't be worth a broken guitar pick. Dig?"

"I dig."

"Now, here's how I can help you. Number One: I can get you off the hook with Uncle Sam. On my say-so, the narcotics charge gets dropped and the other charges never get filed. As far as the United States Government is concerned, you remain an A-Number-One-First-Class Citizen. Clean. Clean as a whistle. Number Two: I can get you off the hook with The Big Head and the rest of your comrades. So far, no one but me knows that you said a word about the conspiracy. Play along with me, and that's the way it'll stay. Sound good?"

"Sounds good."

"Now here's what you can do for me. I know a lot about The Big Freak-Out, but I want to know a lot more. You can tell me everything you know. Then, when you've told me, you can find out what else I want to know. I'll see to it that you're protected, but you've got to play straight with me. And you've got to play straight right up till the end. Cross me just once and I'll throw you to the dogs." I paced the floor long enough to let the message sink in. "Is it a deal?"

His eyes were glued to his feet. His arms were draped across his knees, and his hands were nervously kneading each other. "Damon," he said softly, "what you're asking me to do is turn fink on my buddies."

"Precisely."

"You're asking me to be a stoolie, Damon. And a spy."

"I couldn't've put it better myself."

"You're asking me to go back on all the principles I believe in, to turn traitor to my cause, to sell out!"

"Exactly."

He looked up at me. "You're really being rough on me,

110

Damon. You're really being rough."

"Yep. Now what's your answer."

He stood and walked slowly to the cell window. His fingers clutched at the bars and his knuckles went white.

"Well?" I prodded. "What's your answer?"

"You know my answer. What else can I say? You're holding all the cards."

I patted him fraternally on the shoulder. "I know what you feel like, chum. This is the same way *I* got into the spy business. Now let's adjourn to someplace more comfortable, and fast. We've got a lot of things to talk about and I want to get you out of here before any of your chums realize where you've been."

Marbello brought us to a conference room on one of the upper floors of the building and managed to scare up a tape recorder. Egbert didn't like the idea of putting his words on tape, but I insisted. I wanted Walrus-moustache to have something concrete to show to that Cabinet officer who seemed convinced that The Big Freak-Out was just something we spy-types had dreamed up to keep ourselves busy. I explained my thinking to Egbert, and he consented. The machine whirred to life. We began talking.

"When did all this Big Freak-Out jazz start?" I asked.

He shrugged. "Your guess is as good as mine. I've heard stories, but I don't know anything for sure."

"Let's talk about some of the stories."

"Well, from what I hear, the whole idea was Swami Swahili's."

"The Black Muslim?" I remembered the name from my conversation with Chiquita.

"Yeah. He and The Big Head were great buddies for a while. They used to turn on together every night, and Swami used to have a part in the show at The Church of the Sacred Acid. He used to be on stage with The Big Head and Chiquita during the love demonstration bit. They played the race angle, I guess—showing everybody how

111

love transcended color and creed."

"And The Big Freak-Out was his idea?"

"Yeah, that's the way I hear it. Like I said, he and The Big Head used to turn on together every night. According to what I hear, they used to sit around talking about what a great world this'd be if everybody loved everybody else and all that The Big Head always used to say that if he could persuade everybody in the world to try acid just once there'd never be any problems because everybody'd suddenly discover how important love was and they'd all put aside their materialistic hang-ups and get down to the essentials It was the sort of thing he's always talking about But of course he didn't have any idea about how to make it happen. Then one night Swami came up with the idea."

"You mean polluting the Washington water supply?"

"More or less. At first he wasn't quite so practical about it. He and The Big Head talked about polluting the oceans, or polluting all the rivers in the world, or dropping the stuff into clouds so the rainfall would be polluted. You know, stuff like that, all very impractical. Then Swami said something like, 'Man, we can never pull off this kind of jazz Why don't we put our heads together and come up with something we can really pull off?' So they put their heads together, and Swami, being a Muslim and having a pretty militant way of looking at things, figured out the bit about polluting the Potomac and staging a coup while Washington was freaked out. Anyway, that's the way it was explained to me."

"What happened next?"

"I don't know. I guess they talked about it for a while with a lot of different people, because I heard about it—and this was long before anybody asked me to be a part of it."

"How did you hear about it?"

"I was at a party one night and Swami and The Big Head were there. As usual, everybody was talking about acid and how the world would be a lot better off if everybody took it. Then Swami said something about polluting the Potomac. He didn't say it that the plan was actually in the works. He just mentioned it as though it'd be a great idea. Everybody agreed with him, then we started talking about something else."

"When was the next time you heard the subject being brought up?"

"A few months later when The Big Head asked me to join in on the plot."

"He asked you personally?"

"Yeah."

"What did he say?"

"He said something like, 'Remember that jazz Swami Swahili was talking about one night? That business about getting Washington freaked out and staging a coup? Well, we're going to go through with it. You want in?' I still didn't think they were serious, and I didn't really care too much one way or the other. But I must've been high or something because I said yes."

"What happened then?"

"Nothing. Not for a while anyway. When I said yes, The Big Head said he'd talk to me later. Then we went our separate ways and I forgot all about it. A couple of weeks later he looked me up and started talking about it again. I was sober this time, and I told him that I really didn't want to get involved. But he kept after me. He saw me every day for nearly a month, and he kept talking to me about it. The more he talked, the better I liked the idea. I mean, let's face it, Damon, the country *is* screwed up. I mean, there's the Black Power thing and the Vietnam thing and the riots and the income tax surcharge and all that crap. I figured that *any*body'd be able to run things better than the joker we got

113

in The White House now—Jeez, I shouldn't've said that on tape. The bastard's liable to hear it and I'll get shot. Erase it, will you?"

I stopped the tape and maneuvered the reel back to the point where he was saying, ". . . the better I liked the idea."

He resumed, "Anyway, I got interested. Like that Oliver Wendell Holmes cat said: if a guy doesn't get in on the action and the passion of his time, he hasn't lived. I figured, what the hell, the world is going to pot, I might as well take a shot with this thing and see if I can do something to make life better for the next guy, you know what I mean?"

I nodded. "So you joined up with The Big Head. What happened after that?"

"We had meetings. Lots of meetings. We were the meeting-est bastards in New York."

"Who attended the meetings?"

"The people who were in on the thing."

"For example?"

"You want names?"

"Every one you can remember."

"Jeez, it's hard to remember who was in it way back then and who came in later. Let's see. There was The Big Head, of course. And his mistress. And——"

"His mistress? You mean Chiquita?"

"No. This was before Chiquita came on the scene. He had another mistress then. Her name was Francine."

"Where is she now?"

"I don't know. She faded out when Chiquita faded in. I heard she went out on the coast somewhere."

"Okay. Back to the meetings. Who attended besides The Big Head and Francine?"

"Well, there was Swami Swahili, of course. And Dave Price—he's a guy who runs a bookstore on East Eighth Street. And a guy named Louie, from Boston. I never got his last name. And a guy named Jimmy, from Philadelphia. I didn't get his last name either. And a guy named Manny

Holland. He lives up on Seventy-Third Street. And. . . ."

He reeled off a dozen more names, none of which meant anything to me. I had him identify each person as precisely as he could, knowing that Walrus-moustache would chase down all the leads as soon as the tape was in his possession. Then I asked what was discussed at the meetings.

"The big problem at first," Egbert replied, "was figuring out how much acid we'd need to dump in the water supply and how to keep it from evaporating before the people drank it. The Big Head said he'd get together with some professors he knew back when he was teaching school and see what he could find out. Eventually he came up with an estimate of how much stuff we'd need. But we still were nowhere near figuring out how to keep it from evaporating. And another problem was where to get the LSD. The Big Head had good contacts, of course, and he could buy it a lot cheaper than any of us could. But the amount we figured we'd need would cost more than ten grand, even at the rate The Big Head was paying for it."

"How were these problems finally solved?"

"I don't know. All I know is that one day I went to a meeting and found that none of the old crowd were there anymore. There were only five or six guys, and The Big Head explained that we were going to hold our meetings in smaller groups from now on for security reasons. He told me that he had set up a plan of attack for the coup and that I was going to be part of a platoon that knocked off the Treasury Department. The platoon leader was going to be a guy named Ray Devaney, an economics professor from one of the colleges The Big Head used to teach at. When our crowd finally took over, Devaney'd wind up as Secretary of the Treasury. Another guy was going to be the Commissioner of Internal Revenue, another guy the chairman of the Securities Exchange Commission, and so on. I was just going to be one of the flunkies. I felt pretty put out about this, especially since I'd been in on the plot

115

from almost the beginning. But when I said so to The Big Head, he just told me to stay cool and not worry about anything because if he wanted to he could leave me out of the deal completely."

"And nothing more was said about how to get the LSD and how to keep it from vitiating?"

"No. I asked The Big Head about it once, and he said not to worry because all that had been taken care of. But he didn't give me any details. After that, the only meetings I attended were the Treasury Department meetings. Ray Devaney taught us the plan of attack The Big Head had set up, and we rehearsed it, using maps of Washington and floor plans of the treasury building. The guys who were going to be big shots in the deal, like the Commissioner of Internal Revenue, studied the duties of the officials they'd replace once they took over. The rest of us just hung loose."

I asked Egbert to spell out the Treasury Department plan of attack. Devaney's platoon, he said, would be quartered in two apartments in Arlington, Virginia. There would be eighteen men in the group, two of whom had already gone to Washington as part of an advance guard. The remainder would get there the day before A-Day. But A-Day hadn't yet been set. The only instructions Egbert had received were to keep prepared because the order to move could be given at any moment and he'd have to be prepared to swing into action immediately.

Next I prodded him for details about the battle plans of the other platoons. He said that he only knew that there were twelve platoons, each assigned to a different governmental department. One was assigned to the White House, and The Big Head presumably was its leader. No one had said so specifically, but it was generally assumed that when the smoke had cleared he would be President. Other platoons were assigned to the Pentagon, the State Department, the Justice Department and other agencies.

Egbert had no idea who was in charge of these units or where they would be quartered or how they would attack.

I asked about the plotters' general headquarters. He replied that the original plan had called for it to be located in Chevy Chase, Maryland, but that the plan might have been changed after the group had been broken down into platoons. He said that since the breakdown into platoons he had communicated only with Ray Devaney and other members of the Treasury Department platoon, and that whenever he tried to discuss The Big Freak-Out personally with The Big Head he had been told not to talk about official business except through the chain of command.

As he spelled out the details of the platoon setup, I could see why he had been so ready to believe that I was one of the conspirators. But I could also see that I wasn't going to get any up-to-date reports on overall strategy from him. Ever since the platoon breakdown, he had been kept in the dark about all matters outside his immediate bailiwick. I shifted the questioning to subjects about which he might be more knowledgeable.

Subject Number One was The Big Head. Unfortunately Egbert didn't know much more about him than I did. After the platoon breakdown, the high priest of The Church of the Sacred Acid and would-be President of the United States had kept his own counsel. He had continued to fraternize with his hippie friends, but he had maintained a studied aloofness.

I asked, "Do you think he's the brains behind the operation?"

Egbert replied, "Not anymore. It might have started as his idea, but it seems to have gotten away from him."

"Do you think he's taking orders from somebody?"

"I don't know, but I doubt that he set this all up on his own. He never was the type of guy to make elaborate plans for things. I think he has a few partners now—maybe the people who staked him for the money to buy the LSD to

117

pollute the water supply, or the people who figured out how to keep the stuff from evaporating before it reaches the people."

"Is he a homosexual?" I asked.

"I don't know, man. He acts kind of swishy sometimes. I heard that he doesn't make it with his mistresses, but he never came on to me. And he never came on to any guy I know."

Subject Number Two was Swami Swahili. Egbert seemed to know only that the Swami had vanished nearly two months ago and hadn't been heard from since. Everyone agreed that the supposed originator of The Big Freak-Out was a talkative guy, and this had led to the speculation that he had been murdered. The speculation was lent force by the fact that half a dozen other talkative hippies who were believed to be conspirators had been murdered in New York and other major cities in recent weeks. However, Egbert had heard from a source he considered reliable that the Swami was presently living on a Caribbean isle called Karlota. The isle was owned by a cult of free-love enthusiasts who had emigrated from the United States and set up a commune there.

Subject Number Three was the murdered hippies. Egbert said that he knew none of them personally and only one of them by name. However, he was convinced that all of them were connected with the plot and had been murdered because they talked about it. He recalled that after the second of New York's victims had died, Treasury Department platoon leader Ray Devaney had told him that "this is what happens to guys who can't keep their mouths shut."

Subject Number Four was the last New York garrote victim, James Hartley. Egbert said that he hadn't known who this most recent victim was, only that a fourth New Yorker had been garroted. He added that he hadn't read the newspaper accounts of the crime and that the name

118

James Hartley, which he heard for the first time from me, didn't ring a bell. I asked if he thought he might be able to identify Hartley from the photograph which had appeared in the newspapers, and he allowed that he might. I made a note to get him a copy of the photo as soon as possible.

Subject Number Five was Corinne LaBelle. I described her and pointed out that I remembered her as the one girl at the LSP party who hadn't undressed. Egbert said that he remembered a girl who fit my description at the party and who hadn't undressed while he was around. But the name Corinne LaBelle didn't mean anything to him, and the girl he had seen at the party wasn't one of the regulars among the Sacred Acid crowd. I made a note to obtain the photo of Corinne which Walrus-moustache had shown me and show it to Egbert at the first opportunity.

Subject Number Six was Chiquita. Egbert knew only that she had appeared on the scene about six months ago, that she lived with The Big Head and that she had an insatiable sexual appetite. He said that he had been to bed with her, as had all the other members of The Decline of the West, with the exception of Lola, as had most other males in the Sacred Acid crowd.

Subject Number Seven was Carla. Egbert had seen her with Chiquita only once. She had been introduced to him as Chiquita's sister, but he knew nothing more about her or the other members of Chiquita's family.

Subject Number Eight was Lola. Egbert said that she was "a straight chick" and "a real nice kid." He was positive that she was in no way connected with the conspiracy.

I had no further questions, but I did want to ask all of previous ones over again just to make sure Egbert told the story the same way both times.

I brought him back to the beginning and reworked the same terrain. We rehearsed the origin of The Big Freak-Out, the meetings of the conspirators and the platoon breakdown. Then we went through the cast of characters. There were a few minor discrepancies in his account, but by and large it was the same tale.

For safety's sake I did another rerun. This time I posed the questions differently and tried to feed him confusing leads. He stuck to his guns.

Satisfied that he was telling me the truth, I flicked off the tape recorder. "And now, Egbert old buddy," I said, "let's get down to business. I've got a date this afternoon with Chiquita and another date tonight with The Big Head. I don't know what I'm going to find out, but I'd like to talk to you again after I've seen them. Where should we meet?"

His eyes took on a fearful look. "Jeez, do we have to? I mean, I was with you last night at my buddy's apartment and the night before at The Ink Well. If any of those piano-wire guys happened to be watching, they might put two and two together."

"That's the chance we'll have to take."

His brow furrowed thoughtfully. "Suppose that when I leave here I get hold of Ray Devaney and tell him you've been following me around asking all sorts of questions. He'll think I'm on the up-and-up, and he won't be suspicious if you keep on my tail. Meanwhile, take the names and addresses of two other guys in the Treasury Department group from the tape. You can rough them up, and if you feel like it, you can rough up Ray himself. That'll really confuse the hell out of them."

"For a guy who just became a spy a couple hours ago," I confessed admiringly, "you show a remarkable aptitude for the work."

He grinned. "Well, if you hang around, you gotta learn something."

"Okay, so we'll meet tonight. Where?"

"The Decline of the West is playing at The Rusty Flange on Bleecker Street. Stop in any time between ten and three."

"I'll try to make it, but just in case something comes up and I can't get there by three, where can we meet afterwards?"

"I'm going straight home after the gig. I'll be there until tomorrow afternoon. Then I'm going to Tompkins Square Park for the smoke-in."

"Smoke-in?"

"We've been having them all summer. It's a civil disobedience demonstration against the laws against pot-smoking. There should be a couple thousand people there. If you want to read about what's been happening so far, get a copy of this week's *Tompkins Park Blast*. There's a full-page article on the subject."

I stood up and began rewinding the reel on the tape recorder. "Okay," I said, "I'll see you sometime between the gig tonight and the smoke-in tomorrow. Meanwhile, think back on everything that's happened from the first time you heard about The Big Freak-Out until now. If you come up with anything we missed, let me know about it."

He did a mock salute. "Roger. Anything else, chief?"

"Yeah. Get the hell out of here. I've got work to do."

He scurried out the door. I found the spot on the tape where he had listed the names and addresses of the members of the Treasury Department platoon. I memorized two of them, along with the address of platoon leader Ray Devaney. Then I rewound the reel, put it in an envelope for Walrus-moustache and told Detective Marbello to hold the envelope until his commanding officer told him to release it.

The tape then in good hands, I beelined to a phone booth and placed a call to Aunt Matilda. I briefed her on the latest developments and asked that a photo of Corinne LaBelle be forwarded to me immediately. Then I hailed a cab for the first of the three addresses on the list I had memorized, the address of platoon leader Devaney.

He was a balding, paunchy, middle-aged, horn-rimmed-glasses sort who looked like the last guy in the world anyone would ever suspect of having a part in a conspiracy. His apartment was an inexpensive but well-kept walkup in the West Eighties. I found him sitting on the stoop, smoking a pipe and thumbing through a well-worn copy of *The Economist*.

"Good afternoon, Mister Secretary," I smiled. "How's chances of my getting a job at the mint after you take over."

His mouth popped open and his pipe fell out. He tried to catch it, and in the process, lost his glasses. When he bent to pick them up, two pens and a pencil fell from his shirt pocket. I chuckled at the plight of the blundering bundle of blubber who had allogated to himself the custodianship of the nation's finances. Then, taking advantage of his confusion, I whipped out my wallet and flashed my driver's license under his nose, hoping he wouldn't notice what it really was.

"Detective Marbello, U. S. Marshall's Office."

By the time he had collected his pens and pencil, retrieved his pipe and got his glasses back on his nose, the wallet was back in my pocket. He stared at me dumbfounded.

I said, "We just had a nice long talk down at headquarters with your buddy, Worthington Matthew McGee, alias The Big Head. He spilled all the beans. We knew you were a pinko, Devaney, but we never thought you'd get hooked up in something like this. What happened to your smarts? You should know better than to play games with a bunch of acid-heads. Or are you on the stuff yourself?"

His fat face was shaking like an electric vibrator. The glasses slid down his nose, and the hand with which he tried to readjust them trembled so badly that he finally gave up the effort and let the specs lie where they were.

"I know my constitutional rights," he sputtered. "I

won't make any statements until I've had an opportunity to confer with my lawyer."

I brought my index finger to his nose and pushed the glasses back up to his eyes. "You'll have plenty of opportunity. I'm not going to arrest you just yet. You're more valuable to me running loose. I've got your phone tapped, and I want to get the names of all your buddies when you call them to report what's happening."

"Evidence obtained by a wiretap," he said lamely, "is not admissible in court."

"What a shame. But it'll be fun listening in on your calls anyway. Bye, now. And give my regards to all the other freaks in The Big Freak-Out."

He was still shaking like a leaf when I turned the corner and ducked into the subway.

My next stop was a well-kept garden apartment in what used to be the hangout of the Roaring Twenties' equivalent of today's hippies—Greenwich Village. The man I was calling on was the would-be Commissioner of Internal Revenue, Sanford Weiss.

He wasn't there, but his wife was. She said she'd give him the message.

"Tell him Antoine came by," I drawled. "I'm one of his buddies in The Big Freak-Out."

She looked at me as if I were speaking a foreign language.

"Y'all might not know what that means, Mrs. Weiss, but you just tell Sandy and Ah'm sure he will. Tell him that Ray Devaney sent me. Ray said to tell him that The Big Head blabbed to the cops, and there's gonna be arrest warrants out for all of us. Ray thinks you and Sandy oughta get out of town as soon as y'all can."

I turned on my heel and left her as speechless as I had left Ray Devaney.

Stop Number Three was a roach-infested dive in the

123

East Village, just two blocks from my own pad. The man I had to see was a scraggly, bearded type named Jeremy Slaitt. His profession was sculpting—or so said the sign on the door. Actually he welded together bent scraps of metal and other debris, then sold the crap to people who'd buy anything that *Time* said was "in."

I found the metal-bending Mr. Slaitt in his "studio"—meaning the unfurnished living room of his three-room apartment. The door was open and he was hard at work bending an automobile exhaust pipe, one end of which was imbedded in a pail of cement.

I knocked on the doorframe. He looked up with a scowl and said, "Whatcha want, man?"

"I wanna talk, man," I replied evenly.

He turned back to his exhaust pipe. "So talk," he said.

I crossed the room and positioned myself alongside him. "I like people to look at me when I talk."

He didn't look.

"I *said*," I repeated, "I like people to look at me when I talk."

He still didn't look.

"What do you know about The Big Freak-Out, Slaitt?" I asked.

He looked.

I promptly hauled off with a right cross that sent him somersaulting through one of his latest creations, a conglomeration of steel and other junk built around a rusty alto saxophone and labeled "Ode to Bird Parker."

I was on top of him before he could get to his feet. My fingers clutched at his adam's apple. My knees pinned his biceps to the floor.

His face turned red. I squeezed harder on his adam's apple.

His face turned purple. He thrashed around with his feet a few times. I squeezed harder still, and he stopped thrashing.

124

I loosened my grip. "Start talking," I said.

He gasped for air. "What do you want to know?"

"Everything—and I'm not going to let go of you till I hear it."

"I don't know much," he said.

I tightened my grip again.

"O-okay," he wheezed. "I know a lot."

I loosened my grip. "Let's hear it."

But it didn't come out.

Jeremy Slaitt opened his mouth, muttered a few syllables, then went limp. His eyes rolled back under their lids. His head fell to one side.

I brought a finger to his jugular vein. The pulsebeat was strong. He wasn't dead; he'd just fainted.

I got up and brushed off my clothes.

I knew that he'd talk if I waited until he came to, but I could delegate his interrogation to one of Walrus-moustache's other people. Meanwhile, five p.m. was fast approaching, and pretty Chiquita was waiting to play the piano for me.

I hadn't told her that I'd definitely visit her, but the more I thought of it, the better the idea seemed.

With all the action I had generated during the past few hours, The Big Head and his general staff were sure to be making like Napoleon during the last days at Waterloo.

What better way to check up on the results of my meanderings than by calling upon the mistress of The Great Man himself?

CHAPTER 8

How do you like it?" Chiquita asked, leading me into the apartment.

I did a triple-take. Judging from the company she and The Big Head kept, I had expected to find a dingy dive with floor cushions for chairs, an orange crate for a table and four walls plastered with psychedelic posters. Instead, I found a neat and well-appointed two-bedroom apartment complete with wall-to-wall carpeting, ceiling-to-floor drapes, Naugahyde chairs and a baby grand piano.

"I guess," I observed, "that Dr. McGee is among the hippies but not of the hippies."

Chiquita smiled. "Being a hippie is a state of mind, Damon. The accoutrements have nothing to do with it."

My eyebrows arched. "Accoutrements?"

"Yes. You know. Accessories. The clothes, the furniture in their apartments. . . ."

"I know. But what's a girl like you doing using a word like accoutrements? They didn't teach you *that* in your high school English course at San Juan, did they?"

Her smile broadened. "Damon, you're so suspicious! You should've been a spy, not a sex researcher!"

"I happen to be both, remember? A sex researcher for the League of Sexual Dynamics, a spy for the conspiracy of which I'm a part, and which plans to knock hell out of *your* conspiracy if The Big Head doesn't give us a piece of the action."

126

"Not my conspiracy, Damon. The Big Head's conspiracy. I'm just his mistress."

"And when the smoke of battle has cleared, you'll be the First Lady of the Land, right?"

"If The Big Head wants me to be."

"Well, we're making progress anyway. Last night you wouldn't admit that there's a conspiracy."

"I'm still not admitting anything. I'm just not denying it, that's all."

"And you still haven't explained where you learned a word like accoutrements."

She chuckled. It was a high-pitched, tinkling chuckle—very sweet and very sexy. "I probably learned it from The Big Head. He doesn't exactly speak in monosyllables, you know."

"Monosyllables! There's another! My aren't we being sesquipedalian this afternoon!"

"Sesqui—what?"

"Forget it."

She chuckled again and did a neat little pirouette that sent the hem of her minidress swirling up to her hips. I looked closely, but the hem went down again just before I could determine for sure whether or not she was in her usual lingerie-less state. "But let's not just stand here like two strangers," she said. "After all, we're old friends now. Come in and sit down. I'll make you a drink."

I found a chair with its back flush against a wall—the better to stave off a garroting, m'dear—and flopped down in it. "Scotch and soda," I said.

She pirouetted toward the kitchen, and once again the hem of the minidress went swirling. This time it swirled a shade higher than before. I was able to get a quick but tantalizing glimpse of the bottom curves of her unclad buttocks.

They were the size, shape, consistency and approximate color of a pair of golden honeydew melons. It occurred to

127

me that Walrus-moustache's people ought to put the bite on the national panty-manufacturers' association to subsidize the cost of the campaign to foil the hippies' plot. If the hippies actually got into office, the manufacturers would find themselves with loaded warehouses.

But I had more on my mind than panty-wearing.

For example: piano wire.

I could tell from the way Chiquita was pirouetting around that she didn't plan to let the afternoon pass without a little sex-play.

What better time for a guy with a garrote to put The Big Squeeze on me? If I happened to be on top of her when we were making it, he could get me before I even had a chance to see what he looked like.

Not that I really *cared* what he looked like. But I'd have to make sure I was completely safe before I let my guard down.

Chiquita came back from the kitchen carrying two drinks. She handed me mine, then did another bottom-revealing pirouette and raised her glass in a gesture of toasting. "Here's to sex, Damon. Your business and my pleasure."

It was a stale line, but I decided not to make an issue of it. "To sex," I echoed, hoisting the glass to my lips.

Then I stopped short. I couldn't help wondering if Chiquita had spiked my drink. It was a hokey bit I knew, and no self-respecting spy would dream of really using it, but I tipped the glass upward and faked a swallow, keeping my lips shut. Lowering the glass and feigning uneasiness, I said, "Chiquita, this drink tastes kind of funny."

She regarded me uncertainly. "What do you mean?"

"I don't know. It just tastes funny."

"I used J & B scotch and Canada Dry soda water. It should be all right—unless maybe the glass was dirty. Here, give it to me. I'll make you another one."

"No, don't do that. Just taste this one."

128

"Huh?"

"Taste it, Chiquita." I thrust the glass at her.

"But why don't I just make you another one."

"Taste it!" I snapped. "Now!"

Her brow furrowed. Then her face broke into a glowing smile. "Oh, for heaven's sake, Damon! Do you think I poisoned your drink?"

"Just taste it."

She took the glass, brought it to her lips and polished off a third of it with a single swallow. "There!" she said, handing it back to me. "Now you can drink it without worrying." Pouting prettily, she added, "I've heard of lousy manners, Damon, but yours are ridiculous."

"Better safe than sorry," I clichéd.

She flashed a grin that said all was forgiven, then threw herself into my lap. The firm hemispheres of her un-pantied buttocks sat expertly on my manhood. She gave a little wiggle to let me know that the positioning hadn't been accidental. "Now that you're not suspicious of me anymore," she purred into my ear, "why don't we play awhile? Or would you rather hear me play the piano first?"

Actually I was very much in the mood for play, and not of the pianistic variety, but I still wasn't convinced that I should let my guard down. "Before we do anything," I suggested, "how about giving me a grand tour of your apartment?"

She wriggled again. My manhood got the message. "Certainly," she cooed. "Let's start with the bedroom."

"Okay. But remember, I want to see the whole place, including the closets and behind the draperies and under the beds and anywhere else a guy with a strand of piano wire might be hiding."

"Boy, you are suspicious. And you've really got a fetish for piano wire. I told you before, Damon, the only piano wire I own is in my piano. Take a good look at it. None of the strings are missing."

129

"I'd still like a grand tour of the place. You know, sort of to put me in a more relaxed mood."

She sighed exasperatedly. "You're impossible, Damon. I never met a more suspicious man in all my life." Then she grinned. "But I'm in the mood, and if it takes a grand tour of the apartment to get you in bed with me, I'll give you a grand tour of the apartment."

I made it a really grand tour. I started in the bedroom, then worked my way through the two bathrooms, the kitchen, The Big Head's study and the living room. I checked behind every drape, under every bed, in every closet and over, below, around and behind anything else that might concal a human body. I locked each window and bolted the door. Then I stacked some pots and pans in front of the door just in case someone should unbolt it silently while I was busy in the bedroom.

"You don't miss a trick, do you?"

"I try not to."

"Okay, so now we're safe and sound." She smiled. "Come on over to the piano. I want to play for you."

My eyes did a quick tour of her body. The hem of her miniskirt was hovering provocatively at mid-thigh. The long, luscious legs beneath it were begging to be kissed and caressed. "Let's play beddie-bye first," I suggested. "You can play the piano later."

Her lips pursed up in a sexy little gesture of resistance. "Piano first, bed second."

I glanced at my watch. "Look, Chiquita. It's almost six. I've got a date with The Big Head at seven, and I don't believe in keeping people waiting."

"Don't worry about your date with The Big Head. He told me to tell you that you don't have to show up. He spoke with his partners, and their answer is yes. They're going to cut you in on The Big Freak-Out."

I gulped. "Why didn't you tell me before?"

"You were too busy making me taste your drink and looking behind draperies."

"Well, what else did he say? When do I get to meet with everyone to work out the details?"

"The day after tomorrow."

"No sooner?"

"They can't make it before then. Some of them are in different cities, and they've got a lot of things to keep them busy. But the day after tomorrow all the principals in the plot will fly to Washington. You're supposed to come here to the apartment the same afternoon. Bring all your partners with you. The Big Head will meet you at two, and all of you can fly out to Washington together. The meeting will be at eight that night, and you and your group can come back to New York with The Big Head right after it's over."

I whistled under my breath. I had expected that my little power play with The Big Head would have produced some results, but I hadn't dreamed that things would be handed to me on a platter.

Or *were* they being handed to me on a platter?

Maybe not.

Suppose The Big Head and his people had something up their sleeve?

Suppose that when my partners and I arrived at the apartment we found a reception committee waiting to gun us down?

It would be easy—if we were suckers enough to show up all together in the same place.

Or suppose that The Big Freak-Out had been timed to break the day after tomorrow?

My crowd and I would be in New York twiddling our thumbs while The Big Head and his people were taking over Washington.

I masked my misgivings and favored Chiquita with a

131

grateful smile. "It looks like your pal really set things up for me good. I think I'll stop by The Church of the Sacred Acid tonight and thank him personally."

She smiled back. "You don't have to. I'll give him your message when he gets home."

My smile broadened. "No, I think I'll stop by The Church anyway. You see, I have to work out a few more details with him."

Her smile broadened. "You don't have to, Damon. You can tell me what you want worked out and I'll arrange it for you."

My smile got even broader. It was rapidly becoming a grimace. "I think I'll stop by The Church anyway, Chiquita. You see, there are a few complications and I have to get answers about them now. I don't have time to work through an intermediary."

She stopped playing the smiling game. Her eyes found mine. Her voice was low and even. "The Big Head isn't the only person who can give you immediate answers, Damon. I'm working very closely with him on this thing. You might say that I have his power of attorney."

"I thought you said last night that you didn't meddle in his business affairs."

"That was last night. Today I'm telling you otherwise."

I grinned sardonically. "Maybe I'm just an overly suspicious type, Chiquita, but I get the impression that you're trying very hard to keep me away from The Church of the Sacred Acid tonight."

She grinned back. "How could I do that, Damon? I have to be there myself, remember? I'm part of the show." Then suddenly her grin vanished. "No," she said softly, "I was lying. I *am* trying to keep you away—not away from The Church, but away from The Big Head. As you might realize, you gave him quite a scare last night. He's a peaceful man and not at all accustomed to violent treatment. He was trembling for hours after you left. That's

132

why he arranged the meeting for you. His partners were reluctant, but he talked them into it. You see, he's frightened to death of you." Her hands found one of mine and she squeezed it desperately. "That's why I don't want you to see The Big Head tonight. I don't want him to become upset again. You may not know it, but he has a heart condition. Another shock like the one last night could kill him." Her eyes pleaded with me. "Stay away from him, Damon. Please. I'm begging you. Stay away."

The story obviously was as phony as a pair of falsies. It left me more determined than ever to make my date with The Big Head, but I didn't let Chiquita know what I was thinking. "Okay, I'll leave him alone," I said. "Now let's work out the details."

She leaned against me, and her fingers grabbed me. They worked gently up and down, while her breasts pressed lovingly against my chest. "Okay, Damon. What do you have in mind?"

"Sex," I said suddenly. "No, strike that. What I mean is, if you keep on fingering me that way, I'm going to stop thinking about the conspiracy for a while."

"Okay, stop thinking about it. I'd rather think about sex."

"But if I stop thinking about the conspiracy, we won't have our details worked out before it's time for you to leave for The Church of the Sacred Acid. Then you'll miss your performance, and——"

Her hand was off my manhood before I could finish the sentence. "You're right," she said. "Let's work out the details. But first let me get us a couple more drinks."

She pirouetted into the kitchen and returned with a fresh Scotch-and-soda for me and a gin-and-something for herself.

"Shall I taste yours first?" she asked.

I nodded.

"Damon, Damon, Damon. You're so suspicious. Sooooooo suspicious." She hoisted the glass to her mouth and polished off half of it with a single gulp.

"Thirsty, aren't you?" I quipped.

"Just trying to show you that my heart's in the right place."

It was a cornball stunt, but I couldn't resist it. My hand cupped her left breast, and I grinned and said, "It's in the right place."

"The details, Damon. The details."

I released her. "The details."

We sat on separate chairs—the better to concentrate, m'dear—and I thought up a few details for us to work out.

"It's unnecessary," I began, "for my partners to be brought in on the meeting. I have authority to speak for them, and I can make a firm decision on any question that may arise."

"No good, Damon. They have to attend. The Big Head's partners are frankly very skeptical that you have partners. They think you're a free-lance operator trying to horn in on their caper. Unless they meet your partners, they won't talk."

I stared at her, astonished. The Chiquita I now was talking to was as different from the Chiquita of a few minutes ago as I was different from The Big Head. Somehow or other, once we had started talking business she underwent a strange transformation not only of attitude but also of appearance. Her sexiness was gone. In its place was the hard look of a cold, calculating female executive.

I put on my best executive manners. "But," I argued, "if I were a free-lance operator, all they'd have to do is garrote me. Their troubles would be over."

"True," she replied coldly. "And they haven't discounted that possibility. What it boils down to right now is that they don't know whether or not you're bluffing, and unless

134

you give them some indication of the cards you're holding, they're liable to call your bluff."

"They'd be playing with fire if they did."

"And you'd be playing with fire if you forced them to. Show one or two of your cards, Damon. That way no one will have to call anyone's bluff."

My astonishment continued to grow. Chiquita certainly knew how to handle herself. I'd met a lot of Puerto Rican immigrants in my time, but she was the first recent-arrival in the batch who acted as though she could hold her own in the board room of any corporation in the country. I became more and more suspicious of her alleged immigrant status.

"Okay," I said, "you win. I'll produce my partners. But, like your partners, they're scattered all over the country. It would be pointless for them to come to New York en route to Washington. Why don't we just set the meeting for Washington and let everyone get there by the most direct route."

She smiled. Not her warm, effervescent smile of old. Rather, a cold, thin-lipped smile that was strictly business. "I'll accept that. Arrange to meet with your partners somewhere in Washington a short time before the meeting with The Big Head's partners. The Big Head and you can pick them up wherever they happen to be and bring them to the place where our—The Big Head's partners will be."

I let the our-his slip go by without comment. "Why can't we just designate a meeting place and let everyone arrive there on his own?"

"You're a security-conscious fellow, Damon. Surely you realize that The Big Head's partners have to take certain precautions also. How are they to know that some of your people aren't being spied on by federal agents? By keeping the meeting place secret, they can insure that no dragnet will sweep them all up at the same time."

135

"But, if my people *are* being spied on, the Feds can pick up The Big Head easily enough now, and isn't he the figurehead in the plot?"

"I'm not at liberty to discuss his role or the roles of other conspirators. Suffice it to say that we want to maintain as tight security as we can. We'll meet you halfway by consenting to a pick-up in Washington rather than in New York, but we won't go any farther."

I noticed that this time she hadn't even bothered to correct the reference to the conspiracy in the first, rather than the third, person. Again I let it pass without comment. I wasn't interested in tripping her up. She'd already done that on her own. It would only hurt my case to call the matter to her attention.

I told her that her proposition was acceptable, then tried to get the meeting scheduled twenty-four hours earlier. She turned thumbs down on the idea, explaining that The Big Freak-Out timetable—which I had claimed to know about back when I was threatening The Big Head—called for certain duties to be performed tomorrow without fail.

I went along with her. Actually I wasn't too concerned with the details anyway. Whether the initial contact took place at The Big Head's apartment or in Washington was inconsequential; my "partners" would be several of Walrus-moustache's agents, and they'd play things the same no matter what the terrain. But I wanted to make a pretense of haggling, if only to justify my insistence upon meeting The Big Head after her and my little tete-a-tete.

I haggled awhile longer. She haggled back. Finally we settled on a plan. I'd meet The Big Head at his apartment; we'd fly together to Washington and pick up my partners; the entire group would then proceed to the secret meeting place of The Big Head's partners; we'd have our conference, then go our separate ways; the date would be the day after tomorrow.

136

The haggling now done, Chiquita shed her businesslike pose as quickly as she had assumed it. Her face broke into a sexy smile. She squirmed deliciously on her chair.

"Well, Damon," she cooed, "are you going to make love to me? Or are we just going to sit here all night and stare at each other?"

I didn't give her a chance to change her mind. I was as hungry for her as she was for me. Leaping out of my chair, I bounded across the room and took her in my arms. Then I charged into the bedroom.

"Like, wow," she gasped. "You really make a girl feel wanted. Do you mind if I take off my clothes first?"

I dropped her onto the bed with a thud. As a matter of fact, the idea of making love to her while she was fully dressed—but of course panty-less—had a certain charm to it. Only a few minutes earlier, wearing these same clothes, she had played the role of the stern, cold businesswoman. It would be exciting for me to warm her up until, still wearing the same clothes, she started begging for what I had to offer.

But I chucked the idea. I had a better one, one that wouldn't excite me a whole lot but that very definitely would excite her.

And I wanted her excited.

I wanted her so excited that no matter what happened during the next few days she'd still thirst for my attentions, and thirst for them so desperately that she'd do anything to get them.

I wasn't being generous. I was just being practical.

From what I had seen while we were haggling, she was much more than a mere functionary in The Big Freak-Out. If the time ever came when I found myself in a tough spot with the conspirators, I'd want every friend I could get, and there's no friend as loyal as a friend that's hot for your body!

137

I sat on the bed alongside her and gently stroked her thigh. "Take off your clothes," I said. "But let me kiss you while you're doing it."

She fumbled with the clasp on her dress. I brought my lips to her knee and began kissing my way upward. The closer I got to the top, the longer I took to get there.

In seconds her dress was off. Per custom, she hadn't been wearing anything underneath it. I glanced up at her gleaming, pink-tipped breasts. My spark of desire, smouldering all afternoon, suddenly burst into flame, but I held myself in check. I had a job to do and I was going to do it right. Ever so slowly, I continued to kiss my way up her thighs. My tongue played across her skin. My teeth bit gently into her firm, smooth flesh.

Her hips began to move in slow, passionate circles. Her legs quivered under my touch. "That's beautiful, Damon," she murmured. "That's soooo beautiful."

I inched higher. The sweet aroma of her excitement tantalized my nostrils. Her soft, silky down brushed against my face. My tongue caressed the contours of her womanhood. She wriggled ecstatically.

"Oh, Damon," she moaned. "Oh, ohhhhhhhhh. . . ."

I worked harder. My tongue darted wildly about her moist, pungent cavern. My finger pressed firmly against the tensed muscle which held it prisoner. Her hips thrashed about wildly. Her legs, thrown over my shoulders, swung like lashes. Her feet pounded against my back.

Finally she couldn't stand it any longer. "Damon," she cried. "Take me. Please take me."

I planned to. But not quite yet. First I had to make a couple of adjustments.

Reaching inside my trouser pocket, I pulled out a small envelope. From the envelope I took a milk-white latex device. It resembled a conventional condom, but there was something highly unconventional about it. In Tibet, where I had acquired it, it is called a *ki-vi-mei*. In American

138

slang, it is known as a French tickler, although most people who know the term have never seen the object which it describes.

Slipping my trousers and shorts over my hips, I fitted the device over my manhood. Its sides were studded with soft but firm rubber nipples, nipples which would rake the insides of my partner, spurring her to heights of excitement she never had dreamed existed. At its tip was a sturdy rubber prong, a quarter of an inch thick and an half inch high; with each thrust it would prod her deepest recesses, awakening sensations of pain-pleasure, igniting a fire that burned but did not consume.

The *ki-vi-mei* in place, I began kissing my way up Chiquita's body. She squirmed all the more furiously as I approached her breasts. Her legs scissored around my waist and sought to draw me to her. "Now, Damon," she begged. "Now."

My tongue toyed with her nipples. They were hard and firm. I nibbled at them, and they grew even harder. "Now," she pleaded. "Now!"

I worked my way over the top of her breasts and onto her throat. Her legs were scissoring furiously. Her fingers clutched at my armpits and tried to pull me upward along her body. I held my ground, stoking the fire that was raging inside her.

"Damon," she begged. "Oh, I love you, Damon! Oh! Please make love to me!"

My lips found her adam's apple, her jaw and finally her lips. Her mouth parted and my tongue plunged inside. She sucked it hungrily, at the same time squeezing harder with her legs, trying desperately to pull me into place.

My fingers played between her legs. She pressed against them eagerly, hungrily. I clutched the prong of the *ki-vi-mei* and inserted it experimentally between her frantically trembling legs. Then I lunged forward, letting her engulf me.

139

Her body exploded in paroxysms of passion. Her hips ground furiously. Her legs coiled and uncoiled around mine. Her fingernails dug into my back. "Ohhhhhhh!!!" she groaned. I've never *had* it like this!!!"

I hammered against her, each stroke driving her higher and higher up the spiral of pleasure. Her breath was hot in my ear.

I speeded things up. A hot cone of passion took form inside me. I drove harder, burying my pillar deep in her hollow. Her sighs grew more and more frantic.

The hot waves of excitement inside me came charging to the surface. I thrust once, twice. The eruption began.

I heard myself groan in ecstasy. At the same time, Chiquita's body arched toward me. The spasms which took possession of her told me that she was sharing the moment. Her fingers tore at my buttocks pressing me to her, pressing as desperately as if they had been trying to stuff my entire body into the pit of her passion.

Then it was over. Slowly her grip loosened. She lay beneath me, panting wildly. Her fingers traced a gentle pattern up and down my back. "Damon," she said feebly. "You killed me. I'm dead."

For minutes we lay there silently, our sweat-slick bodies pressed together, our breathing like the whistling of the wind. Then I remembered my appointment with The Big Head. I got up and went to the bathroom to remove the *ki-vi-mei*.

When I came back, Chiquita was sitting on the edge of the bed. She was wearing a transparent blue shortie nightgown that was so sexy it made me want to do again what I had just done. In each hand she had a drink.

"Here," she said, handing me one. "The pause that refreshes."

"I just had the pause that refreshes," I quipped.

"Well, drink it anyway, and come on with me. I want to play the piano for you."

140

I took a healthy slug of Scotch, then followed her into the living room. I wasn't really too eager to hear her play. But a glance at my watch told me that it was only six thirty. I still had half an hour before my appointment with The Big Head. I decided to humor her.

She sat at the keyboard and ripped off a very sloppy arpeggio. Then she ripped off another one—even sloppier. I didn't know what to make of it. Judging from the commotion she had made about her piano-playing, I had expected artistry just short of Horowitz' or Van Cliburn's. What I was hearing was technique that even a rank amateur shouldn't be proud of.

She ripped off another one. I had to look to convince myself that she wasn't playing with her knuckles. Gazing up at me as if very much pleased with herself, she smiled prettily and asked, "What would you like me to play?"

I was tempted to suggest drums. But I curbed my devastating wit. "Whatever you like," I said.

"Do you have any favorites?" She executed another arpeggio—really executed it.

I took another slug of Scotch. "Not really."

"How about a nice Spanish song?"

"Fine," I said, hoping she picked a brief one.

"How about 'Guantanamera'?"

"Great," I enthused. I knew the tune. It had a thirty-two bar chorus. With luck, my torture would be over in little more than a minute.

She began to play, humming along as she did. It occurred to me that both of us would've enjoyed ourselves more if she'd just turned on the radio. At least that would've left her hands free for other pursuits. We might even have had time to knock off another quickie.

But Chiquita wasn't interested in quickies—not the sexual kind, and not the musical kind either. She played and hummed her way through the first chorus, then began to sing a second. Having nothing better to do, I listened to

141

her and tried to place her Spanish accent geographically.

It wasn't easy. Her A's and I's might have passed for Puerto Rican—or perhaps Colombian. But her R's were closer to Cuban. And so were her N's.

I suddenly realized that her accent had sounded strange to me the previous night at my apartment with Carla. I hadn't thought much about it then because it really didn't seem important to me, but now it was beginning to seem very important. Very important indeed.

She had told me she was a Puerto Rican, the oldest child in a family of five who had emigrated to the United States a year ago.

Everything about her, including the way she spoke and sang Spanish, gave her story the lie.

But why should she want to deceive me about the place she came from?

And if she had deceived me, why not claim to be from a more prestigious place? As she herself had noted, Puerto Ricans enjoyed less status in New York than any other group of Latin Americans.

I was still pondering the matter when she finished "Guantanamera." "Well," she beamed, looking up like a schoolgirl expecting a teacher's pat on the head, "how did you like it?"

"Just beautiful," I lied.

"I'm so glad. It's one of my favorite songs. My mother used to sing it to me when I was a little girl."

"Very interesting."

"Now here's another. It's called 'Dolor'."

Dolor translates as "pain," "grief" or "sorrow." I couldn't think of three words more pertinent to Chiquita's keyboard talents. I sipped my Scotch and tried to think of a way to make a quick exit when her—and my—*dolor* came to an end.

Then suddenly I wasn't so eager to leave anymore.

Without realizing it I had received what appeared to be a

142

very important clue about The Big Freak-Out.

The clue lay in the first song Chiquita had played and in her reaction to it.

"Guantanamera" was an old Cuban folk tune. A "Guantanamera" was a woman who came from the Cuban province of Guantanamo. American sailors stationed at the naval base there often complained that "Guantanamera" was the only song they ever heard the natives sing. After a while it got on their nerves because its simple, legato melody was one which burned into their brains; they heard it and heard it and heard it, even when no one was singing it.

Now here was Chiquita singing it. And she had said that her mother used to sing it to her when she was a child. But why in the world would a Peurto Rican peasant sing Cuban songs to her child?

Maybe, just maybe, because she wasn't a Puerto Rican peasant after all. Maybe because she was a Cuban!

I remembered my night with her and Carla at my apartment.

They had entertained me with what they called a *pasa doble*—an ancient sexual stunt which I had first experienced at a brothel in Havana.

Havana, Cuba. . . .

Two plus two equals four.

Now what does a Cuban girl and a conspiracy to overthrow the United States government equal?

Ever since Walrus-moustache had received reports that the Red Chinese were infiltrating the hippie movement, the big question had been: how?

The obvious answer had been: through the use of Caucasian operatives—either Americans, Europeans or Latins.

But where could the Red Chinese, who never courted the favor of Western nations, recruit such operatives?

Again the obvious answer: in the one country which

143

leaned close to the Red Chinese line—Castro's Cuba.

My mind was racing a mile a minute.

Chiquita had claimed to be a Puerto Rican.

She obviously was as Cuban as Fidel himself.

She had pretended to be merely the mistress of the nominal head of the conspiracy.

She obviously had him eating out of her palm.

Two plus two equals four.

And Chiquita plus the Chinese Reds equals the key to the biggest mystery in The Big Freak-Out.

Or did they?

Somehow I had the feeling that they didn't.

True, everything fit into place.

The only problem was that too many things fell into place too easily.

Chiquita had all but literally fallen into my lap.

She had waltzed into my apartment when I had no reason in the world to suspect her of being anything more than The Big Head's comic relief at The Church of the Sacred Acid, and she promptly had given me reason upon reason to change my mind about her.

Then she and Carla had entertained me with a sexual trick which I—Sexologist Rod Damon, of all people—should easily identify as Cuban.

Without bothering to inquire if I spoke Spanish, she had spoken freely in front of me, giving me ample opportunity to detect her accent.

After her visit to my apartment, which served no obvious purpose in the presumed scheme of things, she had invited me to her apartment to listen to her play the piano.

In fact, she had all but twisted my arm to get me to listen to her play the piano.

Then, when she played it, she selected a song which anyone who knew anything about Cuba would recognize instantly.

Why?

144

What was she trying to accomplish?

She hadn't been pumping me for information.

She hadn't been setting me up for a garroting.

The only thing she received in exchange for the cornucopia of clues she had given me was sex.

A commodity not to be despised, for certain.

But did she need it badly enough to risk revealing her identity?

Risk, hell! She had handed it to me on a platter!

Why?!!!

Possibility A: She was the stupidest secret agent on the face of the earth.

Possibility B: She thought I was the stupidest secret agent on the face of the earth.

Possibility C: She was baiting a trap. But what trap?

I thought about it.

And I thought about it some more.

And then I stopped thinking.

My mind had become incredibly light. It didn't want to think anymore. It just wanted to relax.

Yes, to relax.

To relax way up there in that little corner of the room where all the beautiful colors were.

Ah, what colors!

Greens and oranges and reds and purples.

Yes.

And blacks and blues and browns and grays.

Beautiful.

All so beautiful.

Just like the beautiful music coming from the piano.

The piano!!!

I clenched my fist around the Scotch glass and tried to bring myself back to reality.

I was losing my mind.

I had to be losing my mind if I thought Chiquita's piano playing was beautiful.

145

But what had happened to me?

Why was the room suddenly beginning to spin?

Why was I beginning to feel weightless?

I touched the glass to my lips.

Then I stopped short.

The glass.

The Scotch glass.

Three times during the course of our little visit Chiquita had poured me a drink.

On the first two, I had made her taste it before I did.

On the third, I hadn't.

The third—of which I took a stiff slug before I left the bedroom, another stiff slug when she began to play and an additional sip after "Guantanamera."

What was in the glass?

Well, right now there was still better than half a drink in it.

But what was in the drink?

LSD?

LSP?

Something else? . .

My mind became light again.

It floated toward the ceiling.

I gripped the edge of the piano and tried to regain control of myself.

Chiquita had finished "Dolor" and was looking up at me.

Her pretty pink lips were parted in a small sexy smile.

Her flashing black eyes were twinkling mischieviously.

Ah, yes.

Chiquita.

Chiquita the beautiful.

Chiquita the sexy.

Chiquita the drink-spiker.

My mind had come back down from the ceiling.

But how long would it stay down?

Long enough, I hoped, for me to give the pretty Cuban a dose of her own medicine.

I bit hard against the inside of my cheek.

I knew that as long as I could feel the pain my mind would stay with me.

My free hand—the hand that was gripping the piano—suddenly stopped gripping.

The arm shot out and the fingers clutched Chiquita's pretty throat.

They squeezed.

I thrust the Scotch glass in front of her.

"Drink!" I commanded.

She swung at the glass, trying to knock it out of my hand.

I pulled it away. Then I grabbed her long black hair, twisted a fistful of it into a tight ball and pulled back.

"Open your mouth," I said.

She swung at the glass again.

I twisted her hair harder.

Her eyes squeezed shut, and she screamed. It was a high, ear-piercing scream that tore through the room like a siren.

I twisted harder still.

And harder still!

Tears flooded her cheeks. Her face was screwed up in a grimace of insufferable pain. She opened her mouth.

I urged her head back and poured an ounce of the spiked liquor between her pretty lips.

She tried to spit it out, but I twisted harder and she swallowed.

I poured another ounce.

And another.

And another.

The glass was empty.

I let go of her hair.

She looked at me.

We said nothing.

147

There was no need to.

A minute passed.

My mind started back toward the ceiling again.

I fought hard to stop it.

It wouldn't stop.

I bit my lip.

Hard.

Harder.

My mind came back.

Another minute passed.

Chiquita got up from the piano bench and started toward the bedroom.

I stopped her.

"I have to go to the bathroom," she said.

"So you can puke up the drink? Not a chance."

"I *have* to go, Damon."

I twisted her arm behind her back. "Where's some rope?"

"There isn't any here."

"Rope, string, anything. I want some. Or I'll break your arm." I twisted harder.

"In the kitchen. In the cabinet over the sink."

I propelled her ahead of me. "Take it down."

She opened the cabinet and handed me a ball of twine.

"Back to the living room."

She went meekly.

I maneuvered her into place beneath the piano. Her hands were at one piano leg, her feet spread eagled toward the remaining two.

She didn't resist.

I unwound a length of twine and reached for her wrists.

She still didn't resist.

I positioned the wrists on each side of the piano leg and stooped to tie them.

That's when she resisted.

In a flash, she squirmed out from underneath me, took

148

aim at my groin and let loose with a kick. Had she been a split-second quicker, it would have worked, but I saw it coming and deflected it with my knee.

She scampered out from under the piano and started across the room. I dived at her and caught her ankle. She struggled to free herself. Then, when she couldn't, she swiveled toward me and started flailing at my head with her fists.

I blocked one punch, then another. Then I let fly with one of my own. It was a roundhouse right that caught her on the jaw and laid her out cold.

Unconscious, she was no problem. I dragged her under the piano and repositioned her arms and legs. Then I bound them securely and stepped back to contemplate my work.

But I couldn't contemplate anything. My mind was floating toward the ceiling again.

I bit my lip.
No pain.
I bit harder.
Still no pain.
My mouth had a sweet, sticky taste in it.
Blood.
I stopped biting.
My mind floated higher, and my body went limp. I blacked out.

CHAPTER 9

When I regained my senses, I was lying under the piano with Chiquita. My head was cradled between her breasts. My fist was between her thighs. I was savoring the feel of her—the feel of her body, the feel of her dress, the feel of her hot breath against the back of my neck.

"Make love to me," I heard her say.

I turned and looked into her eyes. It occurred to me that they were the most beautiful eyes I ever had seen. I loved them, and I loved the person they belonged to. I vowed that I'd do anything to make her happy, anything she wanted. She had said she wanted me to make love to her. "Okay," I replied.

She smiled. A beautiful smile. A lovely smile. "But you've got to untie me first."

I contemplated her smile. I loved it so much! It was so beautiful! It was the most beautiful smile in the world! The lips were so full and pretty! Every little line on them was pretty! I wanted to love every line individually! And I wanted to love her teeth! Her beautiful teeth! The most beautiful teeth I had ever seen! I loved them!

"Untie me," she repeated.

Her voice. What a beautiful voice! How I loved to listen to it! It was so beautiful that I wanted to listen to it forever and ever and ever! And I wanted to do whatever it told me to do! "Untie me," it had said. I reached for the twine that bound her wrists.

150

Then I stopped.

Somewhere inside me the part of my mind that still belonged to me was fighting to gain control over the part that had been drugged. Harnessing all the will power I could muster, I forced myself to crawl out from under the piano.

Once I was on my feet I seemed to have more control of myself. Everything around me—the piano, the chairs, the rug, even the particles of dust which I could see on the floor—looked beautiful. But the beauty didn't hypnotize me as Chiquita's beauty had. I could take care of myself—at least for the present.

I glanced at my watch. It was eight fifteen.

Time seemed to have lost all meaning for me; it moved slowly, ever so slowly.

And I could see so clearly.

I saw things I had never seen before.

I saw pores in the walls, and fibers in the windows, and thickness in the rug.

I was seeing not in three dimensions but in four.

I was outside the things I was looking at, but I was also inside them. . . .

I forced myself not to become too involved in the visions.

My mind was working slowly, but it *was* working.

I knew that I had things to do, and that it was important that I do them. I made myself do them.

The first thing I did was collect my tie and jacket.

The second was to put them on.

The third was to leave the apartment. . . .

Out on the street, I hailed a cab for The Church of the Sacred Acid. As it rode along, I found myself getting dizzy. My eyes fixed to the back of the cabbie's head. I stared at the hairs there, loving them all individually.

While one part of my mind focused on what I was seeing, the other part was analyzing what was happening to me. Obviously I was high. Very high. But I didn't know on what.

Probably LSD—tasteless, odorless, colorless LSD, which Chiquita had slipped into my drink.

An LSD high, I knew, lasted for close to twenty-four hours. And there was no way to come down once you were up.

I tried not to let myself get alarmed about being up. It was important, I reminded myself, to retain as much control of the situation as possible. If I got alarmed, I'd be losing control. I concentrated on the back of the cabbie's head and let the other part of my mind resume its analysis.

I had told the cabbie to take me to The Church of the Sacred Acid, I realized, because I had had an appointment there at seven with The Big Head.

I had missed that appointment now. And of course The Big Head wasn't expecting me anyway, since Chiquita had told him that she would discourage me from going there. But I wanted to go to the church anyway. I wanted to see why Chiquita had been so eager to keep me away.

The cab continued toward the church.

The ride was unbelievably long.

The distance, I knew, was no more than five or six blocks.

Yet, it seemed as if I had been riding for hours—and The Church still was nowhere in sight.

I focused on the back of the cabbie's head again, and thought about the LSD which Chiquita had given me.

I wondered how much there had been in my drink.

I remembered Walrus-moustache's having said that two hundred and fifty micrograms were enough to make a person hallucinate and that one milligram could send the most jaded acid-head on a trip to end all trips. The trip I was on seemed mild enough, especially in comparison to my LSP trip the night of the party. So it was safe to assume that Chiquita had given me a relatively small dose. Also, I

152

hadn't consumed the full dose—she had taken more than half of it herself. That meant that, as trips go, I was flying pretty low.

Still, I was flying, and not under my own power. I didn't dare chase down any more leads on The Big Freak-Out. The most I could hope to do was take a quick look at what was happening at The Church of the Sacred Acid, make a quick phone call to Aunt Matilda, and head back to my apartment to sleep away the high—if highs could be slept away.

The cab pulled to a halt at the curb. I fumbled through my pockets, found a dollar bill, paid the fare and stepped outside. A glance at my watch told me it was eight twenty-five. If I guessed right, The Big Head should be just winding up his antimaterialism diatribe and moving into his demonstration of the power of love. It occurred to me that Chiquita wouldn't be on hand to help him demonstrate. I wondered if he'd adhere to the old show-must-go-on tradition and use someone else in her place. Coughing up two and a half dollars for the longhaired creep at the door, I wandered inside.

The Church was packed, as usual. On stage, The Big Head was spouting off about why love was afraid. I realized that he still had the entire antimaterialism bit to go through before he got to the power-of-love demonstration and I assumed that the service had been delayed because of Chiquita's absence. I found a seat in the back of the room and awaited further developments.

Then a curious thing happened. As The Big Head climbed out of the love bag and into the antimaterialism bag, I found myself listening to him intently. His arguments seemed well-reasoned and his thinking lucid.

I clenched my fists and dug my fingernails into my palms. Evidently the LSD was still working. I concentrated on the pain in my hands to keep from getting too carried away by the sermon.

Presently the topic shifted back from antimaterialism to love. "I'm going to show you the POWER of love!" The Big Head was saying. "That's right. the POWER! And the GLORY! And you're going to SEE it! Right HERE!"

He walked to the edge of the platform and reached for a girl. She took his hand and climbed onto the platform with him.

"This is Chiquita," he announced. "She's a girl who's known poverty, a girl who's known suffering. And she's a girl who knows love. Watch, now and you'll see it."

On cue, the girl walked across the front of the platform. But she wasn't Chiquita. She was Carla. I watched her pluck a rose from the bouquet in her hand and toss it into the audience. "Flowers," she said sweetly. "Flowers mean love."

(Ah, yes. Business as usual. One of the players might have been changed, but the game remained the same.)

"You heard her," rasped The Big Head. "Flowers mean love, and Chiquita knows love. Now watch and she'll show you."

I watched. But I was more interested in The Big Head than in his pretty assistant. He seemed nervous to the point of being distraught. His voice no longer had the old, confident ring about it. He was like an aging actor playing a part he was no longer suited for, knowing that he wasn't up to the task and hoping against hope that his audience wouldn't notice. I remembered what Chiquita had said about his having a heart condition. I wondered if it were true. He certainly looked it tonight.

My attention shifted from The Big Head to Carla. She had dropped to her knees and unbuttoned her blouse, displaying the mammoth pair of breasts which less than twenty-four hours ago had been my playthings.

I wondered, Was she really Chiquita's sister?

And if Chiquita was an agent for the Chinese Reds, was she one also?

At my apartment, she had spoken only Spanish.

Would the Chinese send a girl who spoke only Spanish on a mission among English-speaking people?

I tried to make some sense out of it, but I couldn't. Thanks to the LSD Chiquita had slipped me, my brain was working on only one cylinder. I'd contemplate a question, then get so involved in my contemplations that I'd forget the question. I refocused on to the proceedings on stage. Carla had already stretched out on the table and was writhing ecstatically while the audience chanted: "Love! Love! Love!"

The LSD made me want to join in on the chanting, but the straight side of my mind prevailed. I watched silently as The Big Head, holding his microphone aloft, positioned himself between the girl's naked, outstretched thighs.

Then I stopped watching.

Something else, far more interesting was bidding for my interest.

Several rows in front of me, two people—a man and a woman—had got up and made their way through the darkened loft toward the door leading backstage. As they stood beneath the exit sign, a deep red glow bathed the woman's face.

I stared hard, and my breath caught in my throat. The woman was a brunette, the same brunette I had seen at the LSP party, the brunette I had thought was Corinne LaBelle.

As I stared at her, I cursed myself for having let Chiquita slip me a spiked drink. If I were sober, I might have followed her. I might even have been able to snatch her away from the people she was with and spirit her off to Walrus-moustache.

But I wasn't sober, and in the state I was in, I didn't dare try anything funny.

Furious with frustration, I sat back and continued to watch her. Then I couldn't watch her anymore because the

155

lights had gone out. When they went back on, she and her companion had gone—presumably through the backstage door.

I left The Church of the Sacred Acid and beelined for a phone booth. Aunt Matilda answered on the first ring. I filled her in on all the latest happenings. Then I hung up and headed for my apartment.

I didn't quite make it.

Suddenly, as I ambled along the street, the effects of the LSD hit me full force. Holes materialized in the pavement, and I kept falling into them. Each hole was filled with slime. It engulfed me, and the only way I could keep from suffocating was to drink it down.

I drank one holeful, then another, then another. Then I puked all over the sidewalk.

But there were more holes, and there was more slime to drink. Finally I couldn't take it any more. I fell into a new hole and refused to open my mouth. The slime seeped up over my nostrils. I held my breath, and everything went black.

CHAPTER 10

When I came to, my watch read one fifteen. I was lying in a gutter, my face immersed in a pool of my own vomit. The hot afternoon sun was beating down on me. I felt as if I hadn't washed for weeks.

I staggered to my feet and read the street sign on the nearest lamppost. Third Avenue and Eleventh Street. That explained why no one had bothered to rouse me. On this stretch of Third, just a few blocks from The Bowery, there usually are more people in the gutter than walking the sidewalks.

I crawled eastward on what was left of my legs. I was only a few blocks from my apartment, and in the shape I was in, I wanted to make it on foot—if only to air out my mind. The effects of the LSD seemed to have worn off, but I didn't want to take any chances.

At a newsstand on the corner of Second Avenue and St. Mark's Place, I picked up a copy of *The Tompkins Park Blast*, remembering that my newfound ally, Egbert, had told me I could find him at the Tompkins Square Park smoke-in and that the smoke-in was the subject of an article in *The Blast*. I wanted to read up on what I was getting into before I got into it.

Th article was buried deep in the paper under the headline: GRASS APPEARS IN TOMPKINS SQUARE PARK. An overline read, "Police Don't Mow Down Smoke-In."

157

Before leaving the newsstand I read the article.

"Local Grass-Rooters in Tompkins Square Park on Sunday demonstrated with another Smoke-In that if the police are sufficiently outnumbered, nobody gets busted.

"At least, that's what happened when a group of anonymous donors began tossing into the crowd handfuls of marijuana joints. Hundreds of people scooped up the joints and turned on, smoking openly and hiding nothing from observers.

"Turning on, tuning in, and laughing, singing and dancing to a rock band were the orders of the day, and the hippies did it. Others who watched without participating did not register any disapproval.

"Both uniformed policemen and plainclothesmen were among the crowd of several thousand, which was a mixture of hippies, Negroes, Puerto Ricans and other groups from the area's ghettoes. The police watched the proceedings quietly and casually ignored them—perhaps wisely so.

"Probably the lack of arrests in spite of evidence before them stemmed from recent unrest and rioting in ghettoes throughout the city and the nation. Apparently the police had decided not to act unless there was violence.

"Whatever the situation, the hippies in Tompkins Square Park proved that they're actively out to change present laws and make marijuana legal. And they just might do it if further smoke-ins are conducted like Sunday's."

So that was the story on the Tompkins Square Park smoke-in movement—hippies exploiting the ghetto people for the purpose of harrassing the police. It was not exactly my idea of democracy's finest hour, but if I wanted to meet Egbert—in the interests of saving democracy—I'd have to join in with the crowd.

Folding the newspaper under my arm, I hobbled the

remaining blocks to my pad. The dirty brick facade of the dilapidated tenement building had never looked better to me. And neither had the face of the guy standing in front of the building.

He was on the street, surrounded by barricades labeled "Dig We Must." In his hands was a forty-pound jackhammer, with which he had ripped a two-yard-square hole in the pavement. When he spotted me, he turned off the motor, squeezed between two of the barricades and hurried to my side. "Where the hell have you been?" he hissed, tugging the ends of his walrus-like moustache. "We've really been worried about you."

I led the way into my apartment and poured a drink for each of us. "It's been quite a night," I said.

He clucked sympathetically. "Aunt Matilda has kept me posted. I can imagine what you went through."

I took a long, slow swallow of Scotch. It tasted good.

"But," he added quickly, "your efforts haven't been in vain. Thanks to you, we've acquired a wealth of valuable information. Last night I played the tape that you and Egbert made down at the Federal Detention Unit. I also assigned men to interrogate the three conspirators you roughed up—Devancy, Weiss and Slaitt. Combining the results of these interrogations with the material from the tape, we've managed to pinpoint all twelve of the hippie platoon outposts. We now have a twenty-four hour stakeout on the outposts. When the platoons swing into action, we'll be ready for them."

I gulped. "Then The Big Freak-Out has been foiled—right?"

"Wrong. There's always the possibility of a last-minute change of plans that will catch us off guard. Besides, even if we do stop the coup from taking place, the pollution of the Potomac can still go off as scheduled. When that happens, Washington will be immobilized. The Red Chinese extremists, aware that the coup has failed, may then prevail upon the powers-that-be to take advantage of our confusion by launching a nuclear offensive. Chances are good that their advice would be heeded. Remember, the so-called moderates in Red China are moderate not because they like us but because they fear us. With our nation's capital freaked out, they'd have no reason to fear us anymore." He shuddered. "It could be a catastrophe, Damon. A genuine catastrophe."

"But," I argued, "now that we've got all this evidence that the coup actually is in the works, can't we persuade the Cabinet officer in charge of the agency's operations to alert the President and other key figures to what's happening?"

"I'm afraid not. The head of our agency met with the Cabinet officer this morning. The Cabinet officer was given all the evidence that we have. He no longer persists in his notion that The Big Freak-Out is a figment of our imagination. But neither is he convinced that the situation is presently grave enough to warrant bringing it to the President's attention."

"Then what does he plan to do about it?"

"He has done something about it."

"Namely?"

"He's appointed a committee to investigate." He sighed. "The wheels of bureaucracy, Damon, grind exceedingly slow."

I sighed with him. "Then we're right back where we started from?"

"Just about. Unless we can come up with more evidence, incontrovertible evidence, that The Big Freak-Out is both feasible and imminent, our worst fears will have been realized. I'm counting on you to produce that evidence." He took an envelope from the pocket of his shirt. "You told Aunt Matilda you wanted a picture of Corinne LaBelle. Here it is. I hope it accomplishes whatever you want it to. And now"—he stood—"I've got to get going. Lots of luck."

I showed him out the door. Then I showered, changed and broiled myself a thick steak. The steak was the first food I had eaten since before my ill-fated rendezvous with Chiquita. I savored every mouthful.

Feeling like a human being again, I subwayed uptown to the back issues department of the New York *Daily News*. I bought a copy of the issue containing the photo of James Hartley, a photo which, if luck was running with me, Egbert might be able to identify. By this time it was four p.m. I subwayed back downtown to Tompkins Square Park.

The park had a long history as a scene of social protest. During the Civil War, it was the location of the nation's first draft riots, demonstrations against President Lincoln's newly passed law permitting compulsory conscription of citizens to serve in the Armed Forces. During World War I, it was the platform from which opponents of intervention in European affairs vented their spleen. During the nineteen-thirties it was a rallying point for followers of Marx, Engels and Trotsky. And now it was the stage on which the hippies were strutting and fretting their part.

When I got there, they were strutting and fretting in a manner which would have made their social-protest predecessors more than proud. All of a thousand longhairs were milling around the bandshell in the center of the park. They carried signs reading "Up with pot," "Marijuana liberates," "We demand the freedom to smoke," "Pot is safer than alcohol," "Mary Jane for the masses" and "The grass is always greener when you smoke it."

On the west side of the park were several hundred other sign-carriers, along with a platoon of young girls who were handing out pro-pot leaflets to passersby on the street. Between the two principal clusters of demonstrators was an assortment of nearly two thousand unaffiliated hippies, all wandering about aimlessly. No one was smoking

161

marijuana just yet, but the eager looks in the eyes of most of the assembly suggested that light-up time was fast drawing near.

I ambled through the crowd looking for Egbert. When he had first mentioned the smoke-in to me, I had expected a gathering of no more than fifty or a hundred hippies and I had assumed there'd be no problem finding him among them. Now I realized that my chances were pretty slim. In that crowd of close to four thousand look-alike and dress-alike hippies, it was like looking for the proverbial needle in a haystack.

I took one turn around the park, then another.

No sign of him.

I took a third turn and a fourth.

Still no sign.

I took a fifth.

Then, not far from the northeast entrance, I stopped short.

A crowd of several hundred hippies were sitting on the grass around a large elm tree.

They were listening to someone sing and play the guitar.

The someone wasn't Egbert—it was the doll in the miniskirt whom I had made love to at The Church of the Sacred Acid the night I had gone there with Lola!

I inched my way through the crowd and tried to get a better look at her.

She was sitting on the grass with her back against the elm tree and her long, sexy legs folded beneath her. Her chestnut brown hair toppled to her shoulders. One of her bra-less breasts was draped over the body of her guitar while the other peeked out from under the neck of the instrument.

"The ravages of war take their toll on our people," she sang. "The farmboy goes fightin' and never comes back . . ."

I listened closely and tried to place the voice. I was sure

162

that I'd heard it before—just as I'd been sure when I saw her in The Church of the Sacred Acid that I'd seen her before. But I still couldn't figure out when or where.

"The Man in the White House says he's not for evil," she went on, "but killin' is evil and killin's his bag."

I nudged the hippie alongside me. "Who is she, man?" I asked.

He looked at me as though I were a visitor from another planet. "You're kidding, man. You've got to be kidding."

"No, seriously. Who is she?"

"She's Dina Grey, man!" contributed a pimply-faced chick on my opposite side. "Can't you tell? Where you been hiding out all these years?"

So that's who she was! Dina Grey, the well known folksinger, social protester and leftist agitator. And that's why she had seemed so familiar to me. I'd heard her voice on the radio hundreds of times, and I'd seen her picture in dozens of magazines. Now she was also my ex-sexmate. So much for the fringe benefits of being a spy!

I'd've liked to hang around and renew our friendship. But I had more important things to occupy my time—like finding Egbert. I turned a quick about-face and vacated the scene. Her voice followed me: "And the metal-torn face that rips up the child and bites out his heart is crying. . . ."

I did another turn around the park.

Then another.

Then, as I made my way through the ever-thickening crowd of hippies in front of the bandshell, I felt a hand at my elbow.

"Hi, chief," said Egbert. "What's shaking?"

We eased our way out of the bandshell mob and through the considerably less dense congregation on the north side of the park. I handed him the photo of Corinne LaBelle.

"Wow!" he said, his eyes threatening to pop out of his head. "What a set of jugs!"

"Do you recognize her?"

163

He brought the photo to within a few inches of his nose. "Hey, Damon, what's this thing here on her left breast right next to the nipple!"

"A tattoo," I said impatiently. "Do you recognize her or not?"

He gave the picture another look. "Yeah, I think I do."

"Was she one of the chicks at the party that night we turned on with LSP?"

"I think she was. Yeah, she was! She was the broad in the gray dress, the one who wouldn't take off her clothes. I tried to get something going with her, but she wouldn't give me the time of day."

"Have you ever seen her anywhere besides at the party?"

He shook his head. "No. That was the only place."

"You're positive?"

"Yeah. With boobs like that, if I saw her before, I'd remember it."

I took the photo back and handed him the one of James Hartley which I'd clipped from the *Daily News*. "What about this guy? Did you ever see him?"

His eyes widened. "Was this the guy you were telling me about? The guy they killed with piano wire?"

"Right. Do you know him?"

"Sure I know him. He's Jimmy from Philadelphia. One of the first guys in the group. I told you about him yesterday.

My stomach tightened.

My mouth went dry.

Jimmy from Philadelphia. One of the first guys in the group.

James Hartley, the boyfriend of Corinne LaBelle.

My mind was racing a mile a minute.

But it was racing in a million different directions.

When Hartley popped up in New York two weeks ago, his appearance had fit very nicely into the theory that

164

Corinne was in town as a prisoner of the Red Chinese agents who were backing The Big Freak-Out. Conceivably she had managed to leak word to him of her plight and he had come looking for her.

Then he was garroted. That fit the theory too. If Corinne's captors had caught him snooping around, they might very well have decided to kill him.

But an envelope containing fifteen LSD tablets had been found near his body. And I couldn't believe that the killer had dropped them. I had a sneaking suspicion that they belonged to Hartley himself. Suddenly the theory didn't seem so solid anymore.

Then there was the business about Corinne at the LSP party. If she had been a prisoner of the conspirators—or of the Chinese Reds who were supposedly backing them—she almost certainly wouldn't have been there. The theory got shakier.

And so I had brought Hartley's photo for Egbert to identify. I was looking for a new theory—like maybe that Hartley was an acid-head and that the conspirators had got their hooks on Corinne through him.

Now Egbert had identified Hartley as one of the crowd.

Beautiful.

Except for one thing. Timing.

Egbert had said that Hartley was one of the *first* guys in the group.

That meant that Hartley was a conspirator at the same time that Corinne supplied Walrus-moustache with the report about the Chinese Reds infiltrating the hippies. And her report was the main reason the conspiracy was now being investigated by me and by Walrus-moustache's other agents.

If she had been part of the thing from the beginning, why did she blow the whistle on herself and her buddies?

Who's side was she on?

It was possible, of course, that Hartley hadn't brought her in until after Walrus-moustache had received her report.

Still, now that he was dead, why was she staying?

Fear?

I doubted it.

But why else?

I couldn't guess.

Another problem: if the Chinese Communists actually were behind the plot, what was Corinne, a rabid right-winger, doing in their camp?

And even if the Chinese Communists weren't behind it, what had induced her to tie in with, and stay tied in with, the hippies?

The more I thought about it, the more baffling it became.

Finally I stopped thinking and resumed picking Egbert's brains.

"What do you know about James Hartley?" I asked.

He shrugged. "Just what I told you. He was one of the first guys in the group."

My fingers closed around his bicep. "Think hard, Egbert! This is important. He may be the key to the whole business."

"But I told you all I know!"

"Then tell me again! Start right at the beginning and tell me everything you can about him, even if you don't think it's important."

He looked hard at the photo, then handed it back to me. We circled a group of longhairs who were chanting the praises of pot to the accompaniment of a trio of congo drummers. Then I found an unoccupied plot of grass on the periphery of the crowd that was listening to Dina Grey's folk songs, and we sat down.

"Well," he said, "I don't know exactly when I saw him for the first time, but it was pretty early in the game. He was a lot older than the crowd I ran with, so I never really

166

got tight with him. We might've said 'hello' and 'goodbye' and all that, but never anything more."

"How did you know he was from Philadelphia?"

"That's the way everybody talked about him. I mean, we were a pretty informal group. We didn't bother with last names or stuff like that. When you met a guy, you said 'I'm Egbert' and he said 'I'm Jimmy.' If there was more than one Jimmy in the crowd, you told them apart by saying 'Jimmy from Brooklyn' and 'Jimmy from Philadelphia.'"

"Was Hartley especially close to The Big Head?"

"I don't think so. I saw them together a few times, but that was about the extent of it. He certainly wasn't one of The Big Head's real close buddies, like Swami Swahili."

"How often did he come to New York from Philadelphia?"

"All the time. He was here just about every weekend."

"When was the last time you saw him?"

"Just before The Big Head broke the group down into platoons. After that, I only went to the Treasury Department platoon meetings, so I never saw him again."

"Do you know what platoon he was in?"

"No."

A vague feeling of uneasiness gnawed at me, a feeling that Egbert had just said something very significant and that I had missed it.

I ran the last few bits of dialogue through my mind again.

Then again.

But it was no use.

Nothing clicked.

I asked a few more questions about Hartley, then changed the subject to the comings and goings of other conspirators. Egbert reported that everyone he knew was nervous, especially after my visits to Devancy, Weiss and Slaitt. But there had been no word from higher-ups about any change in plans. At last count, all conspirators were

167

still standing by for the call that would swing them into action.

I jotted my address on a slip of paper. "Here's where I live," I told him. "If anything really important breaks, come over and tell me about it. If not, keep your eyes and ears open. I'll stop by your apartment tomorrow or the next day for a routine check."

"Roger, chief," he wisecracked. Then he elbowed through a cluster of sign-carriers and vanished in the crowd.

I sat back and watched Dina Grey. She was just winding up a tune about how tough life is in the Mississippi Delta. It occurred to me that with the two or three hundred grand she made each year singing about the poor folk she could probably buy the Mississippi Delta. But I didn't dwell on the subject. I had more important things on my mind.

Like plotting my next move.

I was scheduled to meet with The Big Head the following afternoon for our flight to Washington to meet his and my partners, but the more I thought about it, the more I was convinced that the date was a setup. Otherwise, why would Chiquita have spiked my drink?

Come to think of it, why *did* she spike my drink?

Obviously to keep me away from The Big Head and The Church of the Sacred Acid.

But why did she want to keep me away?

She had said that she was afraid I'd upset The Big Head.

But now that he acceded to my request for a piece of the action, he had nothing to be afraid of.

Or did he?

No. He didn't.

But maybe, just maybe, Chiquita did.

Maybe Chiquita, who all along had been playing Edgar Bergen to The Big Head's Charlie McCarthy, had suddenly found that His Holiness wasn't quite so maneuverable once the chips had begun to fly.

Maybe she had found that he was weakening, weakening enough to want to throw in the towel. And maybe she was afraid that I'd be the straw that broke the camel's back.

It was an interesting avenue of speculation. But to find out for sure I'd have to get alone with The Big Head. And unless I missed my guess, Chiquita would see to it that I didn't.

I was willing to lay odds that she hadn't left his side from the minute he loosened the knots with which I had bound her to the piano.

All of which meant that I would have to confront him and her together.

What better time than the present?

I got up from the grass and brushed off the seat of my pants. Then I started toward the park's southwest exit.

I never got there.

In fact, I didn't get more than two steps away from the spot where I had been sitting because suddenly I ran into a big blue wall of cops.

Little had I realized it, but while I had been engrossed in my contemplations, Dina Grey and her audience of hippies had whipped out their marijuana and begun their smoke-in.

As a matter of fact, more than half the throng in the entire park had begun sucking on thin, hand-rolled cigarettes.

The *Tompkins Park Blast* article had predicted that the fuzz wouldn't bust three thousand people—and the article had been right. But evidently the cops had planned on snagging a random sample of the smokers, and fate had numbered non-smoking-me among the group.

The big blue wall closed in on me and the hippies, nightsticks at the ready, and we were herded toward the edge of the park.

"Wait!" I told the cop nearest me. "I wasn't smoking anything!"

"Yeah, buddy, I know all about it," he said dryly.

169

"I mean it. I don't even smoke cigarettes. Search me if you like."

"You could've ditched the stuff back there in the grass."

"But I didn't. You're arresting an innocent man."

"Tell it to the judge."

Once the group of us was in a corner, the blue uniforms made their way among us, separating the mass into malleable form. One by one, the hippies—and I—were herded into the paddy wagon. I flopped down on one of the benches, cursing the law of averages that once again had turned against me.

In seconds, the benches were full, but the hippie-prisoners kept pouring in. Some of them huddled in the center of the floor. Others sat on the laps of the bench-sitters.

A tall, red-bearded guy who couldn't have weighed less than two-fifty zeroed in on my lap. I waited until he had started to squat. Then I gave him a sideways shove. He bowled into a cluster of hippies a few feet away, knocking them down like bowling pins. I caught his scowl and gave him one back. Happily, he decided not to pursue things any further.

Then another hippie zeroed in on me. But this hippie didn't have a beard. She had long chestnut hair and a body that wouldn't quit. Cradled in her arms, like a baby, was a guitar. Her name was Dina Grey.

My hands found her thighs and guided her into place on top of me. Her head swiveled around, and her pretty lips parted in a glad-to-see-you smile.

"What's a nice girl like you doing in a place like this?" I quipped.

The wagon lurched forward, then moved out into traffic. Dina draped her legs around the outsides of mine. Her buttocks wriggled deliciously against my ever-rigid rod. "My, my," she purred. "I've heard of virility, but this is something else."

170

Her perfume, the same delicate fragrance that had tantalized my nostrils that night at The Church of the Sacred Acid tantalized them again. She draped an arm over my shoulder. Her lips brushed my cheek. "I'm always like that," I explained. "The technical term for it is priapism."

"I know. I've read your books."

My eyebrows arched. "Then you know who I am?"

"Of course. I recognized you from the photo on your book covers. That's why I made a play for you in The Church of the Sacred Acid."

"Suppose the guy in the church had been someone who just looked like me. What would you have done then?"

She chuckled lasciviously. "Sat back and enjoyed it."

The paddy wagon jerked to a halt at a traffic light. The sudden stop sent all of us occupants sliding forward. Then the wagon lurched forward again and we slid back to the original position.

Dina's hand vanished between her legs and began clutching my trousers. "It's a rough ride," she explained. "I think I'd better hold onto something."

I reciprocated by reaching up under her guitar and clutching her breast. She squirmed delightedly and began working open my zipper.

"Uh, Dina," I managed, "do you really think that's such a good idea? I mean, considering the location and all?"

She threw her head over my shoulder and kissed me sexily on the neck. "The hippies won't mind. They're very open minded about things like this."

"How about the cops?"

"They're all in the front of the wagon." She gave me a low, throaty laugh. "What're you so squeamish about, Damon? You know the old saying—gather your rosebuds while you may."

She had it out of context, but I liked the new context a lot better than the old. Reaching under her blouse with both hands, I cupped the lovely rosebuds at the tips of her

171

firm, round breasts. The nipples popped to life in my fingers.

The wagon stopped at another traffic light. We occupants slid forward again, then slid back as the light changed. "Hey, man," Dina called to the hippie who was crouched in front of her. "Hold my guitar for a minute, willya?" He took it, and with both hands free, she arranged her miniskirt over my thighs. Then she began to hum.

I urged my hips forward on the seat. She arched hers and eased my manhood into place. Then she bore down and engulfed it.

The paddy wagon rolled along. The New York Department of Public Works never had been too particular about the condition of its streets, and the one we now were riding was as bumpy as a tank trail. Each bump sent me deep inside her. I couldn't ask for a more efficient shock absorber.

"How's the ride up there?" I asked.

She didn't have to answer. Her buttocks pounded a wild beat against my thighs. Her tongue licked provocatively at my neck. Her breath was hot in my ear.

The road got bumpier. I felt a warm ball of desire swell up inside me. I squeezed Dina tightly, sending my excitement far up into her. She gasped, and her fingernails dug into my thighs. "Don't stop now," she said.

I had no intention of stopping. Every stroke was bringing me to a new plateau of excitement. The street had smoothed out somewhat, but the furious rhythm of Dina's hips more than made up for the bumps we had lost.

The warmth surrounding my passion became a boiling sea. Shock waves of sensation soared through me. I was fast getting where I wanted to go, and Dina was getting there with me. "Ohhhhhhh." she groaned. "Ohhhhh, baby! I'm going to make it."

All of a sudden the wagon hit another stretch of rough street. Dina and I jounced around like twin riders on a bucking bronco. I reached my boiling point and overflowed into her. The frantic scissoring of her thighs told me that she had made it too.

Neither of us arrived a moment too soon. I was still savoring the last delicious tingles of sensation when the wagon jerked to a halt and its motor sputtered off. A few seconds later the back doors opened. "All right, everybody out!" shouted a husky man in blue.

My hands found Dina's hips and tried to ease her off my pillar. But she stayed right in place.

"Hey!" I whispered hoarsely. "Let's not press our luck!"

"I can't help it," she whispered back. "Look what's in front of me."

I looked.

And I looked again.

What was in front of her was the two-hundred-and-fifty-pound bruiser who had tried for a seat on my lap before Dina usurped his prerogatives. He now was sitting on her lap—or more precisely, on her and my laps. To his left, another bruiser was sitting on the lap of the guy who was sitting on my neighbor's lap. And so it went the whole length of the bench. We were stacked in three tiers.

"Hey!" bellowed the bluecoat at the door. "Didn't you hear me? I said everybody out!"

None of the hippies moved. The wagon was packed tighter than the Lexington Avenue Local at rush hour, and the press of humanity inside it was solidly entrenched.

The bluecoat was getting blue in the face. "What is this?!" he shouted. "Are you bums deaf or what?!"

The bums weren't deaf. They were just being obstinate. "It's an old trick," Dina explained. "They want the cops to carry them out. It'll make for better newspaper pictures."

The cop at the door had had his fill. He raised his arm and waved it. In seconds, a phalanx of bluecoated comrades had come to give him a hand.

They carried the hippies out of the wagon one by one. I

173

was hoping that they'd clear the top tier of lap sitters first. If they did, Dina'd have a chance to slide off me without anyone's realizing what had been going on.

But the cops eschewed the tier approach for one that involved carrying away everyone in order of his closeness to the door. That meant that, unless the carrying officers who wound up with Dina were hopelessly inattentive, the nature of our union was sure to be discovered.

I watched as one stack of hippies, then another, then another was hauled away. It was taking time, but the paddy wagon was being emptied.

Soon a pair of burly bluecoats hoisted the two-hundred-and-fifty-pounder off Dina's lap. A second pair of bluecoats promptly moved into place to lift her off my lap. The moment of the truth arrived.

I'll give Dina credit for trying.

She really tried.

As soon as the bruiser was off her, she slipped off me. Then she hovered over me, the hem of her miniskirt giving me a cover under which I could reach to secretly readjust my trousers.

Unfortunately it was a very mini miniskirt and the cover wasn't quite concealing enough. The cops who had come to carry Dina took one look and knew precisely what was happening.

"Bless us and save us!" rasped the first.

"I never thought I'd see the day!" gasped the second.

"I can explain, officer," I chimed in. "You see, I'm Dr. Rod Damon of the League for Sexual Dynamics, and ——"

"Save the palaver for the judge, buddy," crooned the duo in unison. "Both you and your pretty little friend here are just now being arrested a second time," added the first.

"What's the charge?" I demanded.

"Lewd and indecent behavior in an official vehicle of the New York City Police Department."

174

We were ushered into the stationhouse to be booked. A cop behind the desk took our names and addresses. Then Dina was led off in one direction and I was led off in another. I wound up with two dozen hippies in a cell no bigger than ten feet square.

I glanced at my watch. It was six thirty-five.

I knew that I'd have to act fast if I wanted to get to The Church of the Sacred Acid in time to catch Chiquita and The Big Head before the sermon started.

I asked the cop in the corridor if I could make a phone call.

He smiled politely. "Of course you may."

I waited for him to open the cell door.

He didn't budge.

"Uh—I guess I didn't make myself clear," I fumbled. "What I was trying to tell you was that I wanted to make a phone call. You know what I mean? A call. On the telephone."

He smiled again. "I know what a phone call is, buddy."

"Well, are you going to let me make one or not?"

"I certainly am. It's the constitutional right of every prisoner to make a phone call, and I'd be the last person in the world to deprive you of your constitutional rights."

"Well, how about letting me make it?"

"I will . . . in due time. Meanwhile, just be nice and calm. You've got a long night ahead of you, and you won't sleep well if you let yourself get all upset."

I tried soft-soaping him.

I tried browbeating him.

Nothing worked.

He was determined that I wasn't going to exercise my constitutional right until he felt like letting me exercise it.

Fifteen minutes passed. Another group of hippies was herded into a cell next to ours. Fifteen more minutes passed. A second group was herded in.

Soon it was seven thirty.

175

Then it was seven forty-five.

I remembered how I had prevailed upon Walrus-moustache to have Egbert held incommunicado at the Federal Detention Unit so that I could question him.

I remembered also Walrus-moustache's comment that the American Civil Liberties Union wouldn't like it.

I suddenly required a new respect for the American Civil Liberties Union and due process of law.

Finally, at eight fifteen, a police sergeant came back to the cellblock and announced that each prisoner would be permitted to make one phone call. I scurried to the cell door and made sure I was first in line.

Out at the police sergeant's desk I was asked for the number I wanted to call.

I replied with Aunt Matilda's number in Arlington, Virginia.

"Sorry, pal," said the sergeant. "You're entitled to a local call only."

"But I don't know anybody in town. Let me call Arlington and I'll pay for it."

"Sorry, pal. The law says one local call, period."

"Then let me make my call from a phone booth—a *pay* phone booth."

"Sorry, pal. The law says one local call on *this* phone. And you can't dial the number yourself. We've got to dial it for you."

I tried the soft-soap routine.

Then I tried the browbeating routine.

I might as well have tried flying through the stationhouse roof. The sergeant wouldn't budge.

I glanced at my watch. Eight thirty.

"Look," I said, "I'm a researcher and I'm engaged in a very important project. I'm working very closely with the federal government. If you'd like to check my story, phone Detective Marbello at the Federal Detention Unit. It's

176

imperative that I get out of here as soon as possible. There's a great deal at stake."

"Sorry, pal. You can't get out until bail has been set. And bail won't be set until you show up in court tomorrow morning."

I gulped.

Then I gulped again.

I was sure that Walrus-moustache could cut through the stationhouse red tape if I could get in touch with him, but how could I get in touch with him? The only number I had was Aunt Matilda's in Washington.

I decided to try a longshot. I gave the sergeant, Egbert's number. With luck, he'd be home, and all I'd have to do was tell *him* to phone Aunt Matilda with the bad news.

No luck.

He wasn't home.

"Well," said the sergeant, "when you call a number that doesn't answer, you get a chance to call another number. Anybody else you'd like to try?"

I tried another longshot.

I gave the sergeant Marbello's number at the Federal Detention Unit.

Strike two. The phone was answered, but Marbello was out.

"Well, that's it, pal," said the sergeant. "You've had your call. See you in court tomorrow morning."

I went through the soft-soap routine and the browbeating routine one more time.

No luck.

A lanky man in blue took me by the arm and led me down a corridor to the street. In handcuffs, I was tossed into the paddy wagon along with a full complement of hippies. Then the wagon bumped off to New York's detention center, The Tombs. I was shoved into a cell with three other hippies. I did the only thing I could do under

177

the circumstances. I climbed onto the wooden plank that served as my bed and went to sleep.

I was in the middle of my third nightmare when the cell door was opened and I was dragged out. Two cops led me down a long sun-drenched corridor that opened up into a large courtroom. I was told to sit near the front of the room and wait until my name was called.

Half an hour later my turn came to approach the bench. I noticed that most of the people being arraigned weren't hippies. They were drunks, bums and petty hustler-types. I wondered why I'd been separated from the crowd I was arrested with. Then I remembered. The crowd I was arrested with hadn't been caught with pants at half mast in a paddy wagon.

The court officer read the charges. Disturbing the peace, inciting a riot, resisting arrest, unlawful possession of narcotics, vagrancy, lewd and indecent behavior. Bail was set at two thousand dollars.

Once again I was led back to my cell. A joe-college type wearing a short-sleeved white shirt and horn-rimmed glasses came to interview me. He was from the Legal Aid Society, and he wanted to know if I had a lawyer.

I pow-wowed with him and finally persuaded him to place a call to Aunt Matilda. Then I lay back on my plank to await further developments.

An hour passed.

Then another hour.

Then a third.

Finally, after three and a half hours, a cop opened the cell door. "You can go now," he said. "Your bail has been posted."

Another cop led me through a couple of doors. I found myself in the lobby of the stationhouse. I looked around for Walrus-moustache, all set to give him a piece of my mind for taking so long to come to my rescue. He was nowhere in sight. But Dina Grey was.

178

"I figured it was my fault you got in all this trouble," she smiled, "so I posted bond for you." Her fingers found the collar of my shirt and she straightened it. "Would you like to have lunch with me? You must be starved."

I glanced at my watch. It was three fifteen and I had missed my appointment with The Big Head. There was no telling what else I had missed. For all I knew, the hippies could have polluted the Potomac and swung into action on The Big Freak-Out while I was playing games with the desk sergeant.

I gave Dina a polite but quick brush-off, then dashed into the street.

I realized that The Big Head might still be waiting for me, so I skipped my usual phone call to Aunt Matilda and hailed a cab for his apartment.

Halfway there I changed my mind and told the cabbie to take me to my own apartment instead. The reason I changed my mind was simple. On the seat of the cab was a copy of the afternoon newspaper. The headline was about New York's fifth garrote murder in less than three weeks. Beneath the headline was a photo of the victim.

The victim was The Big Head.

The cab pulled to the curb in front of my apartment. I paid my fare and started up the stairs. Sitting on the first landing was Lola, the love-doll who started it all.

"I've been waiting all afternoon for you," she said. "Egbert told me to get in touch with you. He said it's urgent."

"Where is he?"

"He's in Aruba."

I did a triple-take. "WHERE?"

"Aruba. In the Caribbean. He phoned me from there this morning. He said to tell you that he wants you to fly down there immediately."

"Did he say why?"

"Yeah. He said The Big Freak-Out is ready to go. He's

179

down in Aruba now with Chiquita, her sister and another girl. He's——"

"What other girl?"

"Her name is Corinne LaBelle, he said. I don't know who he means."

CHAPTER 11

Aruba isn't much of an island. Only seventy square miles' worth. Its capital, Oranjestad, is even less of a city. About as glamorous as Hoboken.

But the tourists who flock there in droves twelve months a year aren't looking for glamor or excitement. They come for the climate. And what a climate it is. Annual average temperature: seventy-eight. Annual average low: sixty. Annual average high: eighty-nine. Annual average humidity: sixty-one per cent. Average condition of skies: sunny. Average status of barometer: steady.

When I got there, it was an average day. I clambered down the gangway of my plane and into a scene that could have come straight from a travel folder. The sun was setting, and its deep red rays bathed the airport with soft, mellow light. A gentle breeze whispered through the swaying palm trees. There wasn't a cloud in the sky.

What a change from the bad-weather capital of the world, New York! But I didn't let myself get too wrapped up in the beauty of Aruba, I had more important things to do.

I collected my luggage and hailed a cab for Hotel Ortega, where Lola had said Egbert would be waiting for me. He was—right in the lobby. And he didn't waste time with formalities. "Come on," he said. "We've got four minutes to catch a ferry."

181

We dashed out of the hotel and into the back seat of a waiting taxi. Egbert barked a few instructions at the tiny West Indian driver. The cab shot off.

Silver-trunked palm trees whistled by as we raced down spacious Avenida Garcia Lorca. I glanced at the dashboard. The speedometer registered sixty-five.

"How far is the dock?" I asked Egbert.

His eyes were riveted to the street in front of us. "Another half a mile."

I breathed easier. "We should make it in no time."

He frowned. "Don't be too sure."

The cab turned a corner and I realized why he was being pessimistic. Avenida Garcia Lorca had been a smoothly paved boulevard. The street we just turned into was nothing more than a dirt road, barely wide enough for two cars to pass.

We roared down the road, leaving a sandstorm behind us. The cab bounced like a hopped-up exercycle.

Suddenly the cabbie jammed on his brakes. Just in time. Another cab was coming at us.

We swung to the far right of the road as the other cab maneuvered to the far left. The brush on our starboard side hammered against the windows. Still we had only inches between us and the other cab.

The pass having been accomplished, we picked up steam again. But we just as quickly lost it as we closed in on a man on horseback.

The mangy steed loped along the center of the road as if he owned it. Our cabbie honked the horn. The nag didn't budge. There was another honk. Then another. The horse's rider turned and shook his fist at us. But the horse stayed right on course.

The cabbie tried a flanking maneuver. As if out of spite, the horse angled over to block our path.

The horn honked again, then again. Finally the horse got out of the way and we shot by him, but precious time had

182

been lost. A glance at my watch told me we had only a minute and a half to make it.

The minute and a half wasn't enough. It would have been, except that we encountered a pickup truck. He was going in the same direction we were, but at five miles an hour.

He obligingly moved to the right when he saw us coming. But our cabbie was so eager to roar past him that we went off the road and into a ditch. A minute later we were out of the ditch, and a minute after that we were on the dock—just in time to see the ferry sail gracefully toward the horizon. We headed back to the hotel.

Egbert had booked a double room and thoughtfully furnished it with Scotch and soda. I poured out a healthy one. Then I flopped down on my bed and asked him to fill me in on what was happening.

"They're on Karlota," he said. "That's why we were trying to catch the ferry."

"Whoa," I interrupted. "Who's Karlota? And who's on her?"

He chuckled. "You've got too much sex on your mind, Damon. Karlota's not a she. It's an it."

I remembered my conversation with him at the Federal Detention Unit in New York. He had said that Swami Swahili, presumably the originator of The Big Freak-Out plot, was rumored to be living on a Caribbean isle owned by a cult of free-love enthusiasts who had emigrated from the United States and set up a commune there. The name of the isle was Karlota.

"Okay," I said, "Karlota's an it. Now who's on it?"

"Chiquita. And that broad you showed me the picture of—Corinne LaBelle."

I looked at him incredulously. "And you and I were going there to meet them?"

"Not exactly to meet them. To spy on them."

"How do you know they're there?"

183

"I saw them get on the ferry this afternoon."

"How do you know they haven't left?"

"Because there's only one ferry, and they weren't on it when it came back. It just left again now, and it'll be back at ten." He glanced at his watch. "We have an hour and a half and the next trip is tomorrow morning."

I scratched my head. "This is getting confusing."

"Then maybe I'd better start at the beginning."

He took a long swallow of Scotch, then stared at the ice cubes in his glass. "Things started happening as soon as I got home from Tompkins Square Park. About six thirty a Chinese guy came by my apartment. He said that Ray Devaney wasn't in on The Big Freak-Out anymore and that he was taking over Ray's platoon. I asked him how soon we were going to swing into action and he said in a couple of days. He told me to stand by until I heard from him again. Then he left. I figured you'd want to hear about it right away, so I went to your apartment. You weren't there. I figured you might still be at the park, so I went there. That's when I heard about the arrests."

"How did you know I was arrested."

"I didn't. All I knew was that the cops had picked up fifty people. The guy who told me about it said that Dina Grey was one of the fifty, and I remembered that when I left you you were sitting in the grass near where she was. I didn't have anything else to do, so I went down to the stationhouse and asked about you. The sergeant there said that you'd been busted and that you wouldn't be arraigned until the next morning. I figured you'd want me to keep an eye on things for you while you were tied up, so I went over to The Church of the Sacred Acid to see what was happening."

I smiled. "You've really got this spy game down cold."

He shrugged. "What the hell. You do something, you might as well do it right." He took a long swallow of Scotch. "Anyway, when I got to The Church, it was closed

184

up tighter than a drum. The front door was locked, and there wasn't anybody around. I knew that The Big Head ran a show every night except Monday, and this wasn't Monday. So I figured something was up.

"I tried the back door. It was open and I went inside. The Church was empty, but I heard voices coming from the hallway in the back where The Big Head changes for his performances. I sneaked up to the door and listened. There were three broads talking. I couldn't catch everything they said, but the gist of it was that somebody had messed things up and now the situation was getting out of hand. One of the broads said that Ray Devaney was out of the picture and another guy was taking his place. They mentioned a few other changes too. Then they started putting down The Big Head for not being able to take care of himself. One of them said he couldn't be trusted anymore because he knew too much. They haggled awhile about who could take his place. They must've talked about this for fifteen minutes, and they suggested twenty or thirty different names. But all the guys they suggested were either needed in some other part of the operation or else weren't right for some other reason. Finally one of the broads said something like, 'Why don't we use his lover?' Right away the other two said that this'd be a great idea. Then they started talking about The Big Head again and what they could do with him. Somebody said something about exiling him to Karlota, but one of the other ones wouldn't buy it. She said he should be eliminated. That was her exact word—'eliminated.' And when one of the others put up a squawk about it, the one who made the suggestion said, 'If we could do it with Jimmy, we can do it with Matt.' I guess 'Matt' was what they called The Big Head sometimes."

"Yeah," I interposed. "His middle name is Matthew."

"Anyway, they agreed to knock off The Big Head. Then they started talking about who was going to dump the LSD into the Potomac. The way I understood it, they had this

185

barge somewhere on the river with a big vat on it. The vat contained the LSD, plus whatever chemicals and other things they had mixed with it to keep it from evaporating. According to what this one broad said, the guy who was supposed to dump it originally couldn't do it because they had pulled him off the job to take Ray Devaney's place in the Treasury Department platoon. I guess this meant that the Chinaman who looked me up was the guy who originally was going to dump the acid. Anyway, they mentioned a few other guys they might've tapped to dump the acid, and finally this one broad said they'd use a guy named Chang. There was some discussion about whether he'd be willing to do it. It seemed that he was a very big guy in the operation and that he'd want to stay at the organization headquarters to coordinate things instead of going out to dump the acid. But the broad who first said that they should use him said not to worry about whether he'd be willing, because now that everything was all screwed up he'd have no choice. That settled that matter. Then they started talking about you."

"Me?"

"Yeah, you. One of them said she had sent a guy to kill you, but he couldn't find you. He was still looking. Then the other two started talking about how great you were in bed. They said it'd be a shame if the other broad killed you before she had a chance to rack out with you herself. She made a joke about it and they started talking about different platoon leaders—like who could be trusted and who couldn't. Finally they agreed that everybody could be trusted except the guys in charge of the platoons who were going to take over the Department of Agriculture and the Department of the Interior. One of them said that these platoons didn't really matter very much anyway, and they dropped the subject. Then they agreed to meet at The Church the next morning to fly here to Aruba. There was some talk about whether they should take their private plane or go by commercial jet. One of them said that the private plane would be needed for a trip to the West Coast, so they'd go commercial, but the private plane'd come down for them when it was time to fly back. I could see that they were getting ready to break up the meeting then, so I left the door where I was listening to them and went to a dark corner of the loft where I could watch them when they came out. A few minutes later, the first one came out. It was The Big Head's mistress, Chiquita. A few minutes after that, the second one came out. It was Chiquita's sister Carla. Then the third one came out. It was the broad you showed me the picture of—Corinne LaBelle."

I whistled under my breath. "Three for the see-saw."

"Huh?"

"Skip it. Just tell me this: you're sure you heard all three of them talking?"

"Yeah. I could tell the three different voices."

"But they always spoke in English?"

"Yeah. I wouldn't've understood them otherwise. English is the only language I know."

"Okay. What happened next?"

"I waited a while after they left, just to make sure nobody'd see me sneaking around. Then I took off. I figured you might be interested in what was happening with The Big Head while all this other stuff was going on with the broads, so I went to his apartment. He and Chiquita were there together. I needed some excuse for going there, so I told him about the Chinese guy who claimed he had taken over the Treasury Department platoon and I asked if the guy was on the up-and-up. The Big Head didn't even get a chance to answer me. Chiquita told me that the guy was okay and to do whatever he told me. Then she sent me on my way. I breezed around the East Village for the rest of the night, talking with other guys I knew who were in on the thing. Nobody seemed to know what was happening, so finally I went home and sacked out."

187

"You had a pretty busy day."

He chuckled. "It was nothing. You should've seen what I went through today. At nine in the morning the Chinese guy came pounding on my door. He said The Big Freak-Out was ready to roll. I had twenty-four hours to get myself squared away in New York. Then, tomorrow at nine, I was supposed to fly to Washington and go to the platoon headquarters in Arlington. Everybody had to check in the headquarters by noon, he said, because the LSD was going to be dumped into the Potomac that afternoon and the city'd get it in the water supply the next morning. He wanted all of us in town early just to make sure there were no slip-ups."

I whistled under my breath. "So the stuff is going to be dumped tomorrow afternoon." I glanced at my watch. "We've got just about sixteen hours."

He nodded. "Yeah. Anyway, after the Chinese guy left my place, I went over to yours. You still weren't back from jail. I thought about leaving you a note telling you to get in touch with me, but I didn't want to take the chance that somebody might find it. So I killed an hour, then went to The Church to catch the meeting between Chiquita, Carla and Corinne. I waited in the coffee shop across the street until all three of them had gone inside, then I followed them. The door was locked. I didn't want to take a chance going in through a window, so I went back to the coffee shop and waited until they came out. They came out together this time, not one by one, and they had suitcases with them. They started trying to flag down a cab. I went to the corner of the street, so I could get a crack at a cab before they did. When I got one, I had him pull down to the other end of the street and wait until they got their cab. Then I had my guy tail them. They went to the airport and checked in for the flight to Aruba. I bought a ticket on the same flight."

"It's a good thing you had enough money with you."

188

"Yeah. The Decline of the West got paid for two nights work, and I hadn't given the money to the guys. I hope you can pay me back, or I'll really be in trouble."

"Don't worry, you're on an unlimited expense account. What happened after you bought your plane ticket?"

"I didn't want them to see me get on the plane, because I knew Chiquita would recognize me. I picked a seat in the back of the coach section, then waited for them to board. A few minutes later, I boarded and went straight to the john. I sat there on the throne until we were in the air. Then I went back to my seat and turned toward the window as if I was asleep. I don't think they spotted me."

"You really touch all the bases, don't you?"

"I try. Anyway, after we landed in Aruba, I followed them here to the Hotel Ortega. They took a suite two doors down the hall from this one. I found that out by slipping the desk clerk ten bucks and telling him I had the hots for Chiquita. I hid in the lobby until they came back down. Then I followed them to the ferry for Karlota. When they got on, I checked out the schedules at the ferry office, then came back to the hotel and took this room."

"Why didn't you follow them to Karlota."

"Because I had to let you know what was happening."

"What do you mean?"

"Well, Karlota's a real small and primitive island. I learned all about it some time ago from some guys in the East Village who had been there. It's only about a mile long, and there're no telephones or other contacts with the outside world. The only way you can get on or off it is by taking the ferry. The ferry makes three trips a day. It leaves Aruba at seven in the morning and comes back at nine. Then it leaves again at one in the afternoon and comes back at three. Then it leaves at eight in the evening and comes back at ten. I saw them get on the one o'clock run. Then I came back to the hotel, took a room and phoned Lola to tell you what was happening. At three I went back

189

to the dock to see if they made the return trip. They didn't. So I came back to the hotel and waited for you. Now here we are. You tell me what to do next."

I looked at my watch. It was almost nine. "We'll check out the ten o'clock return trip and see if they're on it," I said. "If they are, we'll make our play then. If not, we'll take the seven o'clock ferry to Karlota tomorrow and try to find them there. Good enough?"

His eyes widened slightly. "There's just one thing I don't understand. What do you mean when you say we'll make our play?"

I smiled. "We'll place them under arrest."

He gulped. "Uh, Damon, ol' buddy, uh, let's see if I understand you. You're saying that we'll arrest them? With guns?"

"If guns are needed, yes."

"But they'll have guns too."

"Perhaps."

"Well, ah, I don't want to be a killjoy or anything like that, but, well, uh, guns aren't my game, you know? I mean, I don't like getting shot at. It's against my religion. I'm a devout coward. So, uh, why don't you just lay some bread on me so I can fly back to the States, okay? Then we'll call it even. You don't owe me and I don't owe you."

My eyes found his. "I need all the help I can get on this caper, Egbert."

He looked away. "Well, uh, I know that. But, uh, well, you see, it's my mother. I mean, I wouldn't care if it was just me, but I'm an only child. And my mother has a heart condition. If anything happened to me, it'd just kill her. You know? So, just give me my bread and let me split, okay? Not for me. For my mother."

I took ten twenty-dollar bills from my wallet and held them in front of him. "Whatever you say, Egbert. I won't try to coerce you."

He took the bills and folded them into his pocket. His
190

eyes were fixed to the floor. For a minute neither of us said anything. Then he looked at me. "Uh, Damon, uh, I don't want to sound fickle or anything, but, uh, do you really think you'll need me?"

"I don't know. But I'd like to have you along just in case I do."

He took the bills out of his pocket. "Well, uh, why don't I just sort of tag along then? I mean, what the hell, we've done okay so far." He thrust the bills at me. "Hold these until it's all over. We'll square the account then."

"What about your mother?" I reminded him.

"She doesn't have a heart condition. She's healthy as a horse. I'm sure she'll bury the both of us."

"If Corinne LaBelle and her chums don't bury us first."

"Huh?"

"Skip it." I shoved the bills back toward him. "Keep the money. You may need it. Then let's have another drink—partner."

He poured two fresh ones and I placed a long-distance call to Aunt Matilda. She promised to have Walrus-moustache phone me at the Ortega as soon as possible. I returned my attention to Egbert and his account of what had happened while I was in jail.

We went through his story twice more, poring over every detail. I was especially interested in the Chinamen who had suddenly entered the picture—the one who had been pulled off the LSD vat detail to take over Ray Devaney's Treasury Department platoon and the other one, Chang, who was now going to man the vat. Egbert didn't know anything more about either of them than he had told me. But I was willing to bet that they had a lot more to do with The Big Freak-Out than vat-dumping and platoon-leading.

Another thing that interested me was the fact that Carla had spoken English during the overheard meeting with Chiquita and Corinne. At my apartment she had pretended to speak only Spanish. Why?

191

And most interesting of all was the sudden emergence of Corinne as one of The Big Freak-Out's top brass. Had she been in on it from the beginning? If so, why had she filed the report about the Red Chinese infiltration of the hippies. If not, what had made her change her mind and decide to throw in with the agents of a country whose ideology was diametrically opposed to everything she ever stood for?

Was it possible that she had been brainwashed?

Possible. A person who had been brainwashed can be induced to do a great many things. But someone else must always be present to do the inducing. Judging from what Egbert had said—especially the bit about "If we could do it with Jimmy, we can do it with Matt"—she was anything but a passive follower.

But if she hadn't been brainwashed, what was her game?

Or possibility number two: could it be that the girl I had thought was Corinne wasn't Corinne after all but someone who merely looked like her? My only means of identification had been a photo, and cameras can play funny tricks.

If the girl wasn't Corinne, the involvement of James Hartley would be pretty hard to explain. But certainly no harder than the involvement of Corinne herself!

It was twenty minutes to ten and the ferry from Karlota was due at the dock at ten. Egbert and I hailed a cab and were waiting for the ferry when it pulled into port. None of the debarking passengers resembled the trio we were looking for so we headed back to the hotel.

Egbert sacked out. I poured myself a tall Scotch and soda, and sat waiting for the call from Walrus-moustache. While I waited, I tried to piece together the loose ends in the case. The harder I tried, the more confusing things became.

Problem number One: Chiquita. She had all but fallen over herself giving me clues that she was a Cuban rather than a Puerto Rican. Why?

192

Problem Number Two: James Hartley. Why had he been killed?

Problem Number Three: The Big Head. He had been killed because he knew too much. What did he know?

Problem Number Four: Corinne. Was she really Corinne? One look at her left breast would answer that question, but with A-Day just hours away, how could I get a look at her left breast?

Problem Number Five: the two Chinamen. If they were Red Chinese agents, how did they get into the United States? If they weren't Red Chinese agents, who were they?

I pondered the problems, but nothing seemed to fit into place. I had the uncomfortable feeling that I was overlooking an important clue—a clue that had been all but dropped into my lap.

I replayed the events of the past week, sifting through every conversation, examining the nuances of every statement.

Nothing seemed to stand out.

I poured myself another drink and did another replay.

Still nothing seemed to stand out.

I began to get drowsy.

My eyes closed, and my muscles relaxed.

I was exhausted.

I wanted only to sleep.

As I lay there, random phrases and sentences fluttered through my mind.

". . . textbook solution . . ."

" . . . The Big Head knew too much . . ."

". . . Guantanamera . . ."

". . . Was this trip necessary? . . ."

". . . Treasury Department platoon . . ."

And then suddenly I didn't want to sleep anymore.

I was wide awake and my pulse was pounding furiously.

I had found my clue.

It had come during my conversation with Egbert at Tompkins Square Park.

I had asked him, "When was the last time you saw James Hartley?"

He had replied, "Just before The Big Head broke the group down into platoons. After that I only went to the Treasury Department platoon meetings, so I never saw him again."

The Treasury Department platoon.

The ideal place for any accountants who happened to be among the conspirators. And James Hartley was an accountant.

But he wasn't in the Treasury Department platoon.

Why?

I had an idea why, and if my idea was on target, it explained a lot of things about Corinne LaBelle.

The phrases and sentences raced through my mind again.

". . . textbook solution . . ."

When I roughed up The Big Head, I hadn't been following the textbook solution. And that threw a lot of people's plans off kilter.

". . . The Big Head knew too much . . ."

Right. He knew what I now knew, and that's why he was too dangerous to be kept alive.

". . . Guantanamera . . ."

The Cuban folk song that Chiquita had sung to me. Chiquita, the ostensibly poverty-stricken young girl. Where does a poverty-stricken young girl get money for piano lessons?

". . . Was this trip necessary? . . ."

Why had Chiquita zonked me out on LSD? So I couldn't meet The Big Head. Why didn't she want me to meet The Big Head? Because she was afraid he'd tell me what he

194

knew. The trip *was* necessary—to keep me from learning who the real people behind the conspiracy were.

I sipped my Scotch and watched all the pieces fall into place.

CHAPTER 12

The telephone rang.

It was Walrus-moustache.

"The Big Freak-Out is ready to go," I told him. "The LSD is supposed to be dumped into the Potomac tomorrow afternoon. The guy who's supposed to dump it is a Chinaman named Chang. He's a Communist. He's a Chinese Nationalist, an extremely *right-wing* Chinese Nationalist, who wants to goad us into war with his Red Chinese enemies. He's working hand-in-hand with Corinne LaBelle. She was in on the deal from the beginning. Her reports of Red Chinese infiltrating the hippies were out-and-out fiction."

"Damon," he sputtered, "where the hell are you?"

"Aruba. Don't you remember? You just phoned me here. Corinne LaBelle isn't far away. She's on an island called Karlota. She and her two aides-de-camp went there for two reasons. One: to get out of New York because things were getting too hot. Two: to pick up the man who's just been tapped to replace The Big Head as the nominal chief conspirator—a Black Muslim named Swami Swahili. According to their plan, Swahili will be the first non-elected and the first Negro President of the United States."

"Damon, you're confusing the hell out of me."

"It'll all be very clear when I get back to the States with my prisoners. I'm going to arrest them tomorrow morning. I'll have them in Washington for you tomorrow night.

196

Meanwhile, get every man you can get your hands on and start prowling the Potomac. There's a barge somewhere on the river that contains enough LSD to turn on the whole city. You've got to find the barge."

"Damon, you must be out of your mind. The Potomac is two hundred and eighty-seven miles long. It starts in the Allegheny Mountains in West Virginia and flows all the way to Chesapeake Bay. There are dozens of barges on it, hundreds of barges, maybe even thousands of barges."

"The one you're looking for has a vat on it. The vat is full of LSD. I'll try tomorrow to find out for you exactly where it is. If I can, I'll get word to Aunt Matilda. If I can't, you're on your own. Bye now."

I hung up the phone and set my wrist-alarm for six. Then I undressed and crawled into bed. I went out like a light the minute my head hit the pillow.

At seven, Egbert and I boarded the ferry to Karlota. Unless I missed my guess, Corinne LaBelle and her contingent would be waiting on the dock when we got there.

They were. Corinne, Chiquita and Carla were decked out in almost identical short shorts and white cotton blouses. With them was a tall, muscular Negro with a nylon stocking wrapped around the top of his head—the badge of the Black Muslim.

Egbert and I waited until they started up the gangway. Then we retreated to the lower deck. When the ferry started moving, we returned to topside. Our quartet of conspirators was standing at the rail, gazing out over the blue waters of the Caribbean.

I didn't want to make a move just yet. The only reason I had made the trip to Karlota was to make sure Corinne and Company were taking the first ferry back instead of the second. Now that I had them in sight, it was time to play a waiting game.

I waited until we docked at Aruba. Then I tailed them down the gangway and back to the hotel. They went

197

straight to their room. Posting Egbert in the lobby just in case they should give me the slip, I went up behind them.

I'll give them credit.

They worked fast.

In fact, they worked very fast.

They hadn't been in the room for more than two or three minutes when I thrust open the door.

Yet, during those two or three minutes, all four of them had managed to shuck their duds and hop into bed.

I found them in a crazy-quilt quadrangle straight out of Marquis de Sade's *La Philosophie dans le Boudoir*.

Swami Swahili was on bottom. His chocolate-colored skin glinted dully against the white bed sheets as he ministered to—and availed himself of the ministrations of—his three comrades.

Chiquita and Carla flanked him. They were lying with their heads toward his feet as they regaled him with the same sort of *pasa doble* treatment they had given me that first night back at my apartment. Their arms were coiled around his legs and their legs were coiled around his arms. His massive hands were between their thighs.

Corinne LaBelle was squatting over his face. His tongue lapped at her while she squeezed Chiquita's left breast with her right hand and Carla's right breast with her left hand.

I stood in the doorway for a moment and watched.

What interested me most was the little red mark alongside the nipple of Corinne's left breast.

It was a tattoo of a heart.

I leveled my forty-five at it.

"Don't anybody move," I said. "The jig is up."

Corinne leaped to her feet like a scared rabbit. Chiquita and Carla just lay in position, dumbstruck. Swami Swahili raised his head and glared at me through red-veined eyes.

"Now look, man," he said, peering over his stick-stiff manhood, "you might have a pistol but that don't give you no license to go around making racial slurs."

"Amendment," I told him. "Strike out 'the jig is up' and read in 'you're under arrest.'"

Chiquita's eyes were a portrait of astonishment. "But, Damon," she cooed, "on whose behalf are you arresting us? I thought you were affiliated with a rival conspiracy."

I grinned. "You knew damned well. That's why you handed me all that crap about your poverty-stricken life. Poverty, my foot. The closest you ever came to poverty was when your daddy took you riding through the slums of Havana back in the days of your leader, Señor Batista."

Corinne's face expressed her surprise. "How did you figure that out, Damon? It was supposed to be a deep, dark secret."

"Now wait a minute." interjected Swami Swahili. "I object to the derogative connation of your adjective, 'dark.' Why couldn't you say 'A deep, light secret'?"

"Oh, shut up," Corinne told him. "You give me a pain."

"I almost didn't figure it out," I told her. "You're a pretty sly fox, Mam'selle LaBelle, but you made the one mistake most sly foxes make. You underestimated the opposition."

"I don't understand."

"I'll tell you all about it on the way back to the States. Meanwhile, first things first." I gestured with my forty-five. "You, Chiquita. Pick up the phone and ask the desk clerk to tell my longhaired friend in the lobby that I want him to come to your room. You, Swahili, take the sheets off the bed and roll them up like ropes. Carla and Corinne, just stand there looking pretty. I'll tell you what I have in mind for you in a minute."

My orders were carried out. A few seconds later, Egbert came bounding through the door. I had him cover the quartet with my forty-five while I used one of the bedsheets to tie Swahili's arms and legs behind his back. Then I used the other sheet to do likewise with Corinne. My belt served to bind Chiquita's arms to Carla's, and Egbert's belt served to bind their feet together.

"Now," I told the thoroughly-tied-up foursome, "I want some answers and I want them fast. If I get them, nobody gets hurt. If I don't, they'll be carrying all of you out of here on stretchers. Question Number One: exactly where on the Potomac is the barge containing the LSD?"

Corinne smiled. "You'd really like to know, wouldn't you, Damon?"

My arm lashed out and the back of my hand caught her across the face. She rolled over on one side, and a tiny stream of blood trickled from her mouth. "You're a good looking head, LaBelle," I told her. "Cooperate and you'll stay that way. Resist and you'll never recognize yourself again the next time you look in the mirror."

"You don't fool me, Damon. You might talk tough. But down deep you're a softie—like all American men."

My arm lashed out again—twice this time. She caught it coming and going. A purple welt took form over her lip. Her cheek began to swell. "Where's the barge?" I asked.

"Suppose I told you? How would you know I was telling the truth?"

"I'd check it. I'm keeping you here in this room until my colleagues back in Washington find that barge. And if they don't find it before the LSD hits the water, you're going to wish you never got into the conspiracy business."

She smiled. "Threats, Damon, threats. But I don't think you're going to carry them out. You see, there's a man standing behind you. He's got a gun pointed right at your back. Unless your hippie friend here drops his gun right now, you're both going to be in very serious trouble."

I chuckled. "Come on, baby. You can't expect me to fall for that gag. It's one of the oldest in the books."

"Don't despise antiquity, Dr. Damon," said a soft male

voice behind me. "Haven't you heard that age is a virtue unto itself?"

Egbert and I swiveled around at the same time. Egbert's eyes popped open and his forty-five fell to the floor. I raised my hands over my head. "You win," I said.

The man in the doorway smiled. His leathery yellow face was crinkled up in an expression of sheer delight. His small slanted eyes twinkled mischievously. His snub-nosed thirty-eight scanned the room like a radarscope. I now realized why it had taken Corinne and her three chums almost no time at all to hop into the sack. They'd been expecting this visitor, and they wanted to knock off a quickie before he arrived.

"Damon," said *la belle* LaBelle, "permit me to introduce Doctor Hsin Tse Long. Doctor Long is a psychologist. He's also a pilot. His plane is presently waiting at Aruba airport for our return trip to the United States. When we get there, I'm going to give the command to release the LSD now waiting in a vat on a barge in the Potomac. Twelve hours later, the city of Washington will be in turmoil. And a few hours after that, the United States will be under the control of my small army of men.

"Orders will go out from the Pentagon for bombers of the Strategic Air Command to launch a nuclear attack on Peking. At the same time, the State Department will advise Chiang Kai Shek that we are fully prepared to support his assault of the Communist-held mainland. China will be returned to the Free World, and the forces of Communist tyranny will have been dealt a mortal blow."

"Just out of curiosity," I asked, "why are you telling me all this?"

She smiled. "Because it is not I who have underestimated the opposition. It is you."

I smiled back. "Don't be too sure about it, honey. My people might not know where your LSD barge is. But we've

201

got the locations of your twelve platoons very carefully pinpointed. They're under twenty-four-hour stake-out right now. The minute your troops swing into action, they're going to march right into the arms of a battalion of U. S. agents, all of whom have been given very strict instructions not to drink any water."

Her smile wavered for an instant, and her eyes took on a worried look. Then the worried look vanished and the smile flashed back on. "I think you're bluffing. But we'll soon find out. Now untie me. And start untying my friends."

I unbound her wrists and ankles while Egbert was releasing Swami Swahili. Then I removed the belts that were holding Chiquita and Carla prisoner. The naked foursome got up and climbed back into their clothes.

"Yes, Damon," said Corinne LaBelle once she was dressed, "I think you underestimated me. And, when we get back to Washington, we'll find out for sure." She turned to the Chinaman with the gun. "Are you ready, Dr. Hsin?"

He bowed politely. "Whenever you are, Dr. LaBelle. But might I ask why you plan to bring these people back to Washington with us. Would it not be far more efficient to eliminate them right here?"

She chuckled. "There's no need to eliminate them. They can't hurt us now, and from what I've heard about Damon, he's a very nice man to have around the house. I think he'll fit very nicely into my future."

Long bowed again. "Whatever you say, Dr. LaBelle." He glanced at his watch. "But we really must be moving. The magic hour draws near."

She bowed back. "Indeed it does, Dr. Hsin. Indeed it does."

When they finished bowing and indeed-ing, they herded Egbert and me out into the hall. Chiquita took my forty-five and guarded Egbert, while Long used his thirty-eight to guard me. We split up into two groups for the cab ride to

202

the airport. Then we united again at Hsin's plane, a sleek, twin-engine private jet that must have cost three quarters of a million dollars.

Hsin closed himself inside the cockpit with his co-pilot, another Chinaman whose name nobody bothered to mention. That left Swahili, the three babes, Egbert and me with the cabin to ourselves. Corinne maneuvered the backs of two of the seats, creating an intimate lounge effect. We strapped down for the takeoff.

The sleek little jet whistled down the runway, then streaked up into the sky. In less than five minutes we were at full altitude.

"Damon," said Corinne, unfastening her seat belt, "I became interested in you when I first read your books. Now that Carla and Chiquita have given me a first person report, I'm more interested than ever. Could I persuade you to give me a sample of your talents?"

I nodded toward my forty-five which Chiquita, seated across the aisle, had pointed straight at my midsection. "I'm not at my best in a tense atmosphere. Do you suppose you could tell her to put the gun away for a while?"

"After what you pulled off in our hotel room? Not a chance."

"Then I guess I'll just have to pass up the demonstration."

She curled her legs up under her on the seat. Her tight white shorts strained under the sexy movement of her hips. Her full, round breasts loomed invitingly beneath the fabric of her sheer cotton blouse.

"Remember," she reminded me, "you're my prisoner. If I give Chiquita the word, you're a dead duck."

I smiled. "If you wanted to kill me, you would've done it back at the hotel."

"True. But the only reason I didn't kill you is that I wanted to enjoy you. If you deny me, I've no longer got that reason."

203

"You've got a point," I admitted. Also, it might be my last chance to get free.

Actually she had two points, both jutting out from her chest like a pair of jet engines. My eyes traced their outline. I reached across the seat and put my hand on her bare thigh. "Shall we adjourn to somewhere more private, or do you like working in front of an audience."

She chuckled. "We can take the front seat. Chiquita'll make sure no one watches us—not that I ever dreamed you'd be bashful."

We made our way to the front of the plane. She slid into the seat, and I slid alongside her. Her mouth found mine. It was open, her lips moist and her eyes closed as she leaned forward. I kissed her gently, her tongue a flickering flame of desire.

Immediately her hand went to my stomach. Her breasts pressed my arm. Then she swiveled around, and placing one knee over my opposite leg, straddled me. Her breasts smothered my face as her hips ground passionately against my belly.

"It's really a lot more fun without clothes," I said.

Her mouth found my ear. "Then take them off, Damon," she whispered. She kept blowing in my ear. Then her tongue flicked into my ears and I almost flew off.

I pulled at the zipper on her shorts. It slid open. My hand eased inside and stroked the smooth, soft flesh of her buttocks. Then I urged the shorts down over her hips and along the splendid columns of her thighs.

Her tongue drew delicious circles on my neck. "Have you loved many women, Damon?" she asked softly.

My fingers undid the buttons on her blouse. "My share, I suppose."

The blouse fell open, revealing a pair of breasts that were not large but perfectly shaped and almost pointed. "How many?"

I buried my face in the center aisle and licked her

creamy flesh. "Ub ub glub," came my muffled reply.

She backed away to give me breathing space. "How many?" she repeated.

"I don't know. Eight hundred, maybe. Nine. A thousand. Why?"

"I just wondered." She brought her breasts back into position. "Most men like to think of themselves as great lovers, but very few actually are. It's nice to meet a man of your experience."

My fingers found its way between her thighs and inched upward. She spread her knees and tried to meet me half way. "Love is an art," I said.

Her mouth was hot and wet against my ear. She arched her hips slightly, slowly enticing my hand. From somewhere deep inside her throat came a soft, sensuous purr. "Would you believe I've never had an orgasm?"

So that was it! She needed some of my expertise.

Dr. Corinne LaBelle, female biochemist, cagey conspirator and would-be scourge of the Western World, was just another chick looking for what it was that most chicks looked for.

My thumb edged between the moist throbbing lips. She lowered her body until immersion was complete. With my free fingers I clutched at the soft, solid sphere of her buttock. She writhed passionately against me. I worked on her gently. This was one firecracker I wanted to go off.

Tipping her over onto the seat, I shook off my slacks. Then, leaning forward, I launched the invasion.

Her hips arched like a bow until the arrow found its target. My mouth closed over one of her breasts. The nape of my neck captured the other. Her body shook with spasms of excitement as we fell into the rhythm of the act. With one hand on each cheek I began to pull her apart as I plunged deeper.

Her hot, steamy insides were like a suction pump. Her breasts strained against my face as I bit her hard, almost

205

sadistically. Her buttocks churned furiously. She threw her head back, and her long brown hair swirled wildly around her.

"Ohhhhh, Damon," she sighed. "Daaaaaaaaaaaamon."

I thrust harder. I could feel the volcano welling up inside me. I wanted to get her to explode with me.

My mouth found hers and my tongue plunged inside. She sucked on it hungrily. Her legs locked around the backs of mine. Her fists pounded my shoulders.

I thrust harder.

Then harder still.

Then it happened.

Corinne LaBelle's body erupted in a paroxysm of mind-bending, nerve-tingling, body-shattering ecstasy.

She gasped as much from surprise as from delight.

Her fingers clutched my shoulders, and her mouth pressed hard against mine.

Her legs were locked around me like steel cables. Her hips ground furiously, striving to milk the moment of every last delicious drop. She couldn't stop. It went on and on. Finally, when it was over, we dressed. Then I followed her to the rear of the cabin, where Chiquita was still sitting stoically with her gun trained on Egbert.

I flopped into a window seat and looked out at the water forty-five thousand feet below us. Corinne sat next to me. Her hand stroked my thigh.

"What did I do wrong, Damon?" she asked quietly.

"Nothing," I murmured absently. "You were just great."

"No, I don't mean sexually. I mean with The Big Freak-Out."

I stared out the window for a moment longer. Then I turned and flashed a grin at her. "Corinne, baby, you did so many things wrong that it'd be easier to tell you what you did right."

She flushed. "I could take offense at that, but I'll let it pass."

206

"Take as much offense as you like."

She pressed her breasts against me and smiled prettily. "Oh, Damon, don't be such a sorehead. We may be on opposite sides, but that doesn't mean we can't still be friends." Her breasts jiggled up and down enticingly. "Seriously, Damon, tell me what I did wrong."

I leaned back in the seat and stretched my legs in front of me. She was asking for a long story, and I wanted to be as comfortable as possible while I told it.

"The key phrase," I began, "is 'textbook solution.' It's a phrase my boss at the agency used when he was discussing the way I bluffed The Big Head about my having a conspiracy that was trying to horn in on his conspiracy. Up to the point when I pulled my bluff, I had a few clues but no conclusions—which was just what you wanted me to have. You knew I was a government agent, and you saw to it that I was fed the clues, and you expected me to act like most undercover agents would."

Egbert suddenly became very interested in the conversation. "Wait a minute, Damon. You mean she actually knew you were an agent and she still fed you clues?"

"Precisely."

"I don't get it."

"Then listen closely. Miss LaBelle is a biochemist, French by way of nationality and extremely right-wing by way of political orientation. She was bounced from the college where she was teaching and finally she had criminal charges filed against her because of her rightist propagandizing. To escape the criminal charges, she fled to Canada and then the United States. She didn't have a passport, and the agency I'm working for found out about her. Under the threat of having her deported, they conned her into taking a few missions for them. Before long she had become one of their top spies."

"I'm glad to see you acknowledge that," she put in proudly.

207

"Anyway," I went on, "before she hooked up with the agency, she was working with a pharmaceutical firm in Philadelphia. While she was there, she met and started dating James Hartley. I don't know too much about the relationship, but in retrospect, it's obvious that they cared enough about each other to keep in touch."

"I was quite fond of him for a while," Corinne put in. "Then I found out what a weak person he was and I lost all respect for him."

I smiled knowingly. "Hartley was a weak person. He was a pothead and later on an acidhead. That's why he came to New York so often. Narcotics and hallucinogens are hard to come by in Philadelphia."

"How did you know he was an addict?" Corinne asked.

"At first I didn't. But after he was murdered the police found an envelope containing fifteen LSD tablets near his body. I couldn't believe that they belonged to the murderer because no man going out on a murder mission would carry his drugs with him. That meant that either they had been lost by someone else who had happened to be in the area earlier or that they belonged to Hartley. Since a guy wouldn't be likely to lose that large a quantity of drugs without looking for them, I guessed that they belonged to Hartley. Then, when Egbert looked at Hartley's picture and identified him as one of the early members of The Big Freak-Out, my suspicions were confirmed."

"He was one of the first guys," put in Swami Swahili with a reminiscent look. "And boy was he an acid-head. He stayed up so much he forgot what it was like to be down."

"While Hartley and the rest of The Big Head's crowd were trying to figure out how to translate their dreams of The Big Freak-Out into reality," I continued, "Corinne LaBelle was in Hong Kong on a mission for my agency. I'm just theorizing, now, but it's my guess that Hartley contacted her with the hope that she, as a biochemist,

208

could help solve the problems surrounding the pollution of the Potomac with LSD. She found out about The Big Freak-Out and became interested in it herself. She was militantly anti-communist and she saw The Big Freak-Out as an ideal vehicle for luring the United States into war with Communist China. She was rather certain that the hippies couldn't overthrow the U. S. Government and operate the country for any length of time, but she felt that the United States could be persuaded into ·hinking that the Red Chinese were responsible for the coup. She hoped that the hippies could hold the city long enough for her to give the order, via the platoon which took over the Pentagon, for a nuclear attack on China and also for her to encourage, via the platoon which took over the State Department, an attack on mainland China by Chiang-Kai-shek's Formosa-based army. But she was hedging her bet. She realized that the immobilization of Washington by the coup might inspire the Red Chinese to launch a nuclear offensive of their own, which the United States, of course, would reply to by bombing mainland China off the map. And she felt that, even if no bombs fell, the United States, believing the coup to be Red China's doing, might revise its policies to the point of taking aggressive action of some sort against Red China, probably through Chiang."

"Sheeet," observed Swami Swahili. "This chick must be really down on them Red Chinese."

"But," I went on, "Corinne soon found that the hippies lacked the organization and stability to pull off the coup on their own. They talked too much and to the wrong people. And they tended to go off on tangents. She had given them a great deal of money—pilfered from the foundation under whose cover she was conducting her Hong Kong spy mission—and she had given them the all-important formula which would insure that the LSD dropped into the Potomac wouldn't vitiate before it was consumed by the people of Washington. Still, the coup wasn't getting off

209

the ground. So she decided to take things in her own hands. That's when Chiquita and Carla came on the scene."

"If I didn't take things in my own hands," Corinne reminded me, "things would still be at the same point as a year ago."

"I don't know where she met them or how," I continued, "but I know they were just as militantly right-wing as she was. Chiquita had dropped all sorts of hints at me that she was Cuban rather than Puerto Rican, because she wanted me to believe she was a Castro Cuban who was infiltrating the hippies on behalf of the Chinese Reds. Actually she was a Batista Cuban, exiled from the island shortly after Castro took power, and she was infiltrating the hippies on behalf of Corinne and—as events later will show—some Nationalist Chinese."

"I met them at a meeting of the John Birch Society," Corinne said. "That was back while I was in Philadelphia. I had kept in touch with them through the years, just as I had kept in touch with James Hartley. They're not sisters, by the way. Chiquita just made that up for your benefit. But your theory is amazingly accurate so far. I'd like to hear more."

"Chiquita came to New York and pretended to be The Big Head's mistress. Actually she was the brains behind the New York operation, pulling the strings while he went through the motions. I don't know whether he accepted her gladly or reluctantly, but I'm sure that her grip on him was quite tight."

"Quite," agreed Corinne. "And he accepted her quite gladly. He couldn't do the job, and he was glad to have someone around who could."

"While Chiquita was in New York," I continued, "Carla was somewhere else—perhaps San Francisco."

"Miami," said Corinne. "I had a different girl in each city. They were all friends who shared my political views."

210

"In any case, the girls ran the show here in the United States and Corinne went about her business in Hong Kong—diverting money from the Coxe foundation, turning in fallacious reports about Red Chinese infiltration of the hippie movement. Also, she established liaison with some extremists among the Nationalist Chinese, who were more than happy to come in on the caper."

"How did you know about that?" Corinne asked.

"The Big Freak-Out required a lot more money than you had been able to pilfer. Since everyone else connected with the operation was low on lucrative contacts, the fund-raising job fell on you. I'm guessing that you approached the most obvious source first and that you got a four-star welcome."

"Right on both guesses."

"Anyway, once the Chinese moved in, the movement became even more efficient. Some Chinese agents came to this country—getting in was easy, since the U. S. honors Nationalist China passports—and went to work behind the scenes. Others stayed in China and conducted fund-raising drives. The Chinese who were here didn't mix with the hippies themselves. But they did coordinate things between the girls who were in charge of the operations in individual cities, and they set up the Washington headquarters."

"Right on all counts."

"They also became very security conscious. Previously, hippies had been rather loose-mouthed about the whole affair. The Chinese promptly put an end to that. Hippies who had taken bad trips and visited public health clinics were garroted. Swami Swahili also might've been garroted as a result of his loquaciousness, except that he was The Big Head's lover and the conspirators feared that they'd lose their grip on The Big Head if his lover was killed. So he was exiled to Karlota and told to lie low until he was sent for again."

211

"I went to Karlota all right," put in Swahili, "but I wasn't no Big Head's lover. What do you think I am, whitey? A faggot?"

"Easy, Swami," cooed Corinne. "There's nothing personal about all this. Go on, Damon."

"It was shortly after the murders that I came on the scene. You learned about me, Corinne, at the LSP party, and when you discovered I was a sex researcher, you suspected that I was spying for the agency. The reason you suspected it was that my cover was so very similar to yours. It was then that you told Chiquita to play up to me and give me clues that she was a Cuban. You hoped to confirm the agency's suspicions, planted by you, that The Big Freak-Out was a communist plot. Chiquita overplayed her part, but of course you had no way of knowing that she was doing so."

"You always were an unsubtle bitch, Chiquita," Corinne chided her goodnaturedly.

"Still, the ploy might have worked. But here's where that 'textbook solution' business I was talking about earlier comes into play. You, Corinne, had assumed that I'd work like most agents would work. You'd assumed that I'd fish around for information and follow up on every lead that came my way. But you never dreamed that I'd try to generate action on my own by bluffing The Big Head about a counter-conspiracy that planned to take over his conspiracy. I bluffed both him and Egbert here, whom I later coerced into telling me everything he knew."

"How did you coerce him?"

"I had him picked up on a Federal narcotics rap, then released on the condition that he'd work along with me. He might not have, except that your Chinese buddies, by garroting talkative hippies, had scared him into thinking that he was damned if he did talk and damned if he didn't."

"Very smart."

212

"When I started playing havoc with your New York underlings, you rapidly called in some of your Chinese pals to reinforce the weak links in the chain. At the same time, Chiquita drugged me to keep me from meeting with The Big Head. I couldn't understand why she wanted to prevent such a meeting, but after you murdered him it became clear. When The Big Head found the Chinese on the scene, he realized that The Big Freak-Out—as *he* had envisioned it—was out of hand. Up until that point, he had been duped into believing that you were supporting rather than controlling him. He also believed that the coup would be successful and that he actually would run the country. Now he suddenly found that he was a figurehead. I think he suspected that the Chinese Nationalists were behind the show. If not, he still knew that he was the tool of a foreign power. And he wasn't at all in favor of a take-over of the United States by an enemy, whether communistic or Fascist. He wanted to *straighten* the country out— distorted though his ideas might have been—but not to *sell* it out. I doubt that he threatened to blow the whistle on you. I think he was too weak for that. But you were afraid that if I kept hammering at him I might get him to crack. That's why you tried to stall me by setting up a fake meeting in Washington involving my partners and his partners. That's why Chiquita drugged me. And that's why you eventually killed him. With what he knew about the way things were going, he was too dangerous to let live."

"Amazing, Damon," said Corinne admiringly. "I never dreamed you'd've figured that out."

"I think that was Hartley's problem too, more or less. I think that Hartley realized what was happening long before The Big Head realized what was happening. I think you suspected that he might go to the police, so you killed him."

"Hartley was weak," said Corinne. "When he learned

213

about the hippies who had been garroted, he said the conspiracy was getting out of hand and that he didn't want any part of it. I think he suspected that the Nationalist Chinese were involved, and for him that was the worst part of all. He was a pinko from way back—even when it was unfashionable to be a pinko. I was sure he'd go to the authorities with what he knew. So I made the decision. He had to be eliminated. He was weak."

"Still," I said, "despite all this, I might not have known the nature of your involvement, Corinne, except for a trivial item about Hartley. You see, when Egbert was describing Hartley's relationship to The Big Freak-Out, he told me that he hadn't seen Hartley since the time when the group was broken up into platoons. Egbert was assigned to the Treasury Department platoon. Why wasn't Hartley, who was an accountant and therefore a logical choice for the platoon, also assigned? I thought about it, and my conclusion was that he wasn't assigned because he occupied a position high in The Big Freak-Out hierarchy, far above the platoon level. Up to this point, I would've been willing to believe that you were an unwitting victim of the conspirators or perhaps that you had been brainwashed by the Red Chinese. But the fact that Hartley was no mere underling meant that you were no mere underling. When I had that figured out, everything else fit into place."

"My compliments, Damon," she told me. "A brilliant job of deduction. There's not much about us that you don't know."

"Only two things," I smiled.

"Which are?"

"The location of your headquarters and the location of the barge that's going to dump the LSD."

She smiled. "Well, naturally you don't know that! Those are top secret!"

"Originally, I know, the headquarters was supposed to be in Chevy Chase. It impressed me as a stupid place to locate, being far out of the center of action. But I suppose you had your reasons."

"As a matter of fact, Chevy Chase was The Big Head's idea. That was before I began drawing up the plans. My idea was for a centralized headquarters, one right in the heart of——"

"Corinne!" interrupted Chiquita, alarmed. "Are you going to tell him where the headquarters is?!"

Corinne chuckled. "Certainly. What does it matter. He can't do anything about it. He's our prisoner."

"But still—"

"Oh, don't be silly, Chiquie. An hour from now he'll see the place anyway. Where else would we hold him prisoner except where we are?"

"If it was up to me," observed Swami Swahili, "I'd give him a bullet right between his faggot white eyes."

"Swami," scolded Corinne sweetly, "is that any way for the future President of the United States to talk?"

"Uh, people," I interrupted, "not to, uh, be rude, but, uh, wasn't Miss LaBelle here about to tell me the location of the conspiracy headquarters?"

Corinne smiled. "Would you believe the Shoreham-Norman hotel, Damon?"

I gulped. "The Shoreham-Norman? But how in the world could you get them to rent to you?"

"Well, silly, we didn't just walk up to the desk and say, 'Look, fellas, we're conspiring to overthrow the government and we'd like to set up headquarters here.' We simply had four very respectable looking Chinese businessmen rent four adjacent suites. Isn't that practical?"

"Very. And I'll bet you even had the good sense to take the penthouse floor—so you'd be way up where nothing could interfere with your radio transmissions!"

"We couldn't get the penthouse," she smiled sadly. "We had to settle for the twelfth."

"Well, something is better than nothing. But if there's

215

radio blockage, how will you get word to the man on the barge in the event that you want to change the prearranged timing of your LSD drop?"

"The timing isn't prearranged. The LSD won't be dropped until I personally give the word at the Shoreham-Norman. I'll merely tell the man who's assigned to the detail that it's time to make the drop."

"Meanwhile, who's watching the acid?"

"It's under guard, of course. But the guards are underlings. I wouldn't trust them with the final responsibility for making the drop."

"Very efficient," I enthused, feigning profound admiration. "And I'll bet your choice of a location for the barge smacks of equal brilliance."

"To be quite candid, I think so too. I've picked——"

But she didn't quite finish the sentence.

No sooner had she begun than the plane went into a steep dive.

All six of us passengers were hurled out of our seats and against the roof.

Then, with a horrendous groan of straining metal, the dive stopped.

All six of us were thrown onto the floor.

What happened next took only a split second.

I saw Chiquita's gun hand lying in the aisle.

My right hand closed around her wrist.

My left pried her fingers from the stock.

I picked up the gun.

And I aimed it at my fellow travelers, all of whom were still so shook up from the dive that they didn't realize fully what had happened.

"Nothing to worry about," came our pilot's voice over the loudspeaker. "It was just an airpocket."

I smiled.

"Egbert," I said, "stand in the aisle here between our

216

friends and the cockpit. If one of them starts toward me, give out a yell."

"Roger, chief," he snapped, moving into place.

I walked to the front of the plane and slid open the cockpit door.

Dr. Hsin turned around. "Nothing to wor—" he began. Then his words caught in his throat as he saw the piece of gleaming steel I had pointed at his face.

"Don't make any sudden moves, Hsin," I told him. "I know how to fly a jet, so I'd shoot you without thinking twice about it."

"Be calm, Dr. Damon," he replied. "Don't get tense, or you might involuntarily tighten your finger on the trigger. I'm a reasonable man."

"Put the plane on auto-pilot," I said.

He did.

"Now both of you put your hands on top of your heads."

They complied.

"Now stand up."

They stood.

I backed into the aisle. "Now come out here one at a time and put your hands against the wall."

They were obedient to the letter.

I took the snub-nosed thirty-eight from Hsin and a .32 Mauser from his copilot. Then I had Egbert tie them up with their belts.

Next I had Swahili and the three girls tied up. Then, giving Egbert the thirty-eight, I retreated to the cockpit.

I'd never flown this specific plane before, but fortunately I'd had enough experience flying Air Force jets that it didn't take long to figure out the cockpit. I took over from the autopilot, got the feel of the plane, tested all my equipment, got my bearings and reset the auto. Then I radioed ahead to Washington that I was coming in with my very hot cargo.

The tower controller balked when I asked him to phone a message to Aunt Matilda in Arlington. But I told him it was a matter involving the life of the President of the United States. He changed his tune in a hurry.

My message was brief and to the point. "Arriving one p.m. with planeload of conspirators. Big Freak-Out headquarters is at Shoreham-Norman, twelfth floor, four suites rented to Chinese businessmen. Don't worry about rates. See you soon. Love, Damon."

The rest was a breeze.

The flight went smoothly.

The control tower let me in without waiting my turn in a holding pattern.

And a trio of police cars rushed out to greet the plane.

I waved triumphantly from my cockpit window at Walrus-moustache and the sexy brunette who was snuggled at his side. Then I lowered the gangway and strode down to meet the cheering throng.

Well, they weren't exactly cheering.

They were just sort of smiling bewilderedly.

And they weren't exactly a throng.

There were just six cops, Walrus-moustache and the brunette.

Ah, yes. The Brunette.

Would you believe Dina Grey?

"What's a nice girl like you doing in a place like Washington?" I quipped.

"Jeez, Damon," she shot back, "when're you gonna learn a new opening line?"

Walrus-moustache cut through our exchange of pleasantries long enough to give me a hearty handshake. "Splendid job, Damon. Splendid job. We raided the Shoreham-Norman and picked up the whole crew. Then we raided the platoon headquarters and got everybody there. All told, there were more than five hundred of them. We don't have jail space to hold them. We've got them quartered

218

temporarily at the National Guard Armory." He shook his head disbelievingly. "More than five hundred of them! I never saw so much hair in my life!"

"Glad to be of help," I said archly. "All of which brings me to the next question: what's a nice girl like Dina Grey doing in a place like this?"

She wrinkled her nose prettily. "I'm on the team, schnook. Our friend here roped me in just like he roped you in. Your weakness was sex, mine was something else."

"For instance?"

"Nice girls don't tell. Anyway, I was on the case in New York just like you were. That's why I introduced myself to you that night in The Church of the Sacred Acid. I stayed pretty close to you after that, but you didn't see me because I just sort of hung in the background. But I was with you every step of the way. It's a good thing I sweet-talked a nasty old matron into letting me make a long distance call, or I never would've got out to scrape up your bail money."

"Well, seeing as how you were in a large part responsible for my getting socked with so high a bail, let's just call it even. Meanwhile, I'll take you up on that luncheon invitation anytime you're ready."

"Like how about tonight?"

"It's a deal."

I was just getting ready to seal it with a kiss when I heard the cop yell.

I wheeled around just in time to see Corinne LaBelle hop behind the wheel of one of the squad cars and tear toward the airport exit.

"She got away while we were bringing the other people out of the plane," the cop alibied.

Another empty squad car was just a few feet away from me. I jumped into the driver's seat at the same time that Walrus-moustache leaped into the back. Dina Grey leaped in right alongside him.

I jammed the car into gear and tore rubber.

Corinne's squad car was rounding the corner of the terminal building.

I flipped on the siren and bore down on her.

She eased through the taxi area and onto one of the feeder lanes. Her siren started wailing too.

Cars ducked out of our path like rabbits ducking buckshot.

My speedometer read fifty, and I had all I could do to stay on the road.

Corinne roared onto the main highway and headed toward the Capitol Bridge.

I stayed with her. My speedometer read eighty, and I was giving it all the juice I had.

She had fifty yards on me, and she kept it.

We roared over the bridge at seventy, then through downtown Washington at fifty-five.

At K Street she made a left.

The traffic was heavy, but it kept moving out of the way.

We dropped to forty-five, and I gained a few yards on her, but I couldn't get any closer.

Down K Street at forty-five.

Through the underpass at seventy.

Over the Key Bridge at fifty-five.

Around the Arlington Circle at forty.

Right turn past the circle at thirty-five.

Back up to sixty on the straightaway.

Then seventy.

Walrus-moustache tugged a forty-five from his shoulder holster and took a bead on her tires.

"Wait!" I said. "Don't shoot! She's going for the acid!"

And she was.

Down to sixty-five for a sharp curve.

Then up to eighty.

Then onto the highway along the river, and ninety.

Ninety-five.

A hundred.

One mile.

Two miles.

Three miles.

Then, wheels squealing like mad, she pulled off the road.

By the time I was parked behind her, she had climbed halfway up the bluff that served as a riverbank.

I took out my forty-five and started after her.

Walrus-moustache and Dina were at my heels.

I fired a warning shot to scare her.

It didn't.

She kept her pace until she was at the top of the bluff.

Then she dived in.

I got to the crest a few seconds after her.

She was tearing through the water, aiming straight for a barge.

On the barge was a vat, painted black.

Surrounding the vat was a scaffold-like construction of stairs and gangways.

Walking one of the gangways was a man with a holstered pistol.

Walking the floor of the barge was another man. He had a shotgun.

The pistol guy saw me first. He got off a shot just as I dived. It whistled over my head.

I heard another shot as I hit the water. I looked up just in time to see the pistol guy go toppling off his perch. Walrus-moustache had got him.

The shotgun guy was raising his gun to his shoulder.

There was another pistol shot.

A small, red hole opened up on his forehead and he crumbled on the floor.

My arms pumped as hard as they could.

Corinne had reached the barge and was climbing on board.

I got there right after she did.

I reached for her leg and missed.

Then I pushed myself over the side as she started up the stairs to the higher of the two gangways.

She was fast.

She got to the top of the stairs just as I got to the bottom of them.

She was halfway across the gangway as I got to the top.

At the end of the gangway was a huge lever.

I didn't need three guesses to know what it was there for and what she planned to do with it.

She made a grab for it at the same time that I threw a flying tackle at her.

My arms closed around her knees and she hit the floor.

But she was up again in a flash.

I grabbed for the lever.

She grabbed for the lever.

I got it.

She got air.

Her arms flailed wildly as she groped for something to support herself.

Then her face froze in an expression of terror as she realized what had happened.

She had lost her footing and was falling backwards . . . backwards . . . backwards into a vat that contained enough LSD to turn on the entire city of Washington, D.C., and its suburbs.

I watched with a sad smile as Corinne went off on the trip of all trips.

Then I started down the stairs.

Walrus-moustache was waiting for me on the shore.

More important, so was Dina Grey.

222